Shaker Town

Book 4 in Taryn's Camera

Rebecca Patrick-Howard

"Oh mother, mother, make my bed
Make it soft and narrow
Sweet William died, for love of me,
And I shall of sorrow."
-*Barbara Allen*, traditional folk song

"Though sad fate our lives may sever
Parting will not last forever,
There's a hope that leaves me never,
All through the night."
- *All Through the Night*, traditional folk song

"Sweet spirits do surround us now
I feel them gathering near.
I can perceive their lowly bow
And hear their heavenly cheer."
-*Celestial Choir*, Anonymous

"Clean your room well; for good spirits will not live where there is dirt."- Mother Ann, Shaker founder

PROLOGUE

*T*he water below was brown and muddy, swollen from

the rain the night before. It rose above the creek bank and lapped at the poplar and spruce trees, threatening to drag them down to its murky depths. Off in the distance the bees buzzed furiously, awake and busy after a long winter. Clusters of daffodils grew in the sunny spots, their bright yellow faces peeping up from the brown, neglected clumps of dirt.

The sobs that escaped from parched lips were dry now, beaten. Most of the tears were long gone and what were left were raspy and slid down cheeks, red and chapped from the salt and wind. It was difficult to believe a person could have anything left after spending most of the night in sorrow.

Loose branches had torn at clothes, leaving them hanging from the body in shreds in some places. A small puddle of blood pooled on the ground and dried, staining the earth with its vulgar shade of red.

They would be coming soon; someone would be there to coax the lost soul back. There would be murmuring, praying, but very little nurturing. What happened when the person was beyond redemption? Beyond saving?

There, caught in the spring breeze, was the light trickle of voices—mostly men. They would be irritated to leave their work, to search for someone who didn't want to be found. But it was their duty and they'd see to it.

There wasn't much time now.

The rocks were heavy and caused tired hands to ache. But they weren't as heavy as the stones in the pocket. Those were the important ones.

Up on the ridge, in the tree line, the voices grew closer. Now the outline of bodies was visible. They'd be there soon, just as soon as they caught the quick flash of fabric in the naked tree branches.

Before another voice could call out, the world disappeared in a flurry and there was nothing but the feeling of soaring through the air, like the bird who sought a taste of freedom. And then, the pull of the water—sweet, dark, and cold.

CHAPTER 1

*T*he spring air was delicious; Taryn could almost taste

the newness. After a bitter, solid winter her skin preened in the
morning sunlight as a light breeze ruffled her hair and softly
lifted it off her neck. Despite her slight misgivings about

returning to an area where she'd almost been murdered, she found herself surprisingly elated at being back in central Kentucky again.

Her suitcase's wheels didn't care for the gravel road, and pulling it across the stones was almost as hard as actually lifting it up and carrying it. A matching pink carry-on bag was slung over one shoulder while her laptop case and purse were balanced on the other side. Her shoulders and back were already aching and she'd pay for that later. She couldn't park very close to her room, however and unless she wanted to make several trips she'd have to grin and bear it—or at least bear it.

Shaker Town was officially called Shaker Village of Pleasant Hill but most people shortened it. All the Shakers were gone now, having dissipated for the most part in the early 20th century, but the park had been restored and re-enactors led tourists through the historical buildings. The Shakers, formally known as the United Society of Believers in Christ's Second Appearing were a mysterious lot, with their loud and eventful worship services, strong work ethic, and tidiness. What set them apart from other religious groups, however, was their unwillingness to either engage in sexual activity or have children—they gained new members through recruiting techniques. And who wouldn't have wanted to live with them in the nineteenth century? In a period when times were tough, the Shakers offered stout, well-made buildings, three full meals a day, heat, and work.

You just had to move in accepting the fact that your husband was now your brother.

4

Taryn was going to be in Shaker Town for a month and was looking forward to every single night. One of the original dormitories and shops had been converted into a small lodging building and she had a semi-suite, complete with small sitting room and large bedroom. Although it included the Shaker-style chairs, bed, and pegs on the wall in which to hang things to keep them organized, it had also been upgraded to include Wi-fi, satellite television, and an iPod charger.

Best of all, she got to eat in the park's restaurant three times a day—for free! She could already taste the mashed potatoes, green beans, homemade rolls, and pie. Pie. Lots of pie. Now, as she lugged her bags up the stairs to the second floor, she was hungry.

The winter was a confusing season for Taryn. She'd spent part of it in Florida with her longtime best friend and sort-of boyfriend Matt, the rest in Nashville at her dinky little apartment. It wasn't much, sure, but it was home and she'd actually enjoyed putting up her sad little fake Christmas tree, tacking stockings on the wall that she filled for herself with things from her favorite stores, and hanging garland over everything that didn't move. She'd inherited all of her parents and grandmother's Christmas decorations and usually just stuck with those, but this year she'd gone to Target and actually bought new ones. On a small table-top tree in her bedroom she'd put up a "themed" tree and hung little snowmen on it. She liked sleeping in her room with the Christmas lights on at night, fire hazard be damned, and was thinking about turning it into one of those primitive trees and just keeping it up year-round. People did that, right? She was almost sure she'd seen it done before.

Matt had wanted her to stay with him in Florida. "Give up your apartment," he'd pleaded with her. "It's just a stopover point for you. You're hardly ever even there anyway."

And he wasn't wrong. It was true that she was rarely home and just used it as a base. But still... it was hers. All her life she'd mostly lived with someone else—first her parents, then her husband, and then with a slab of grief so powerful it might as well have been another person. Now that those things were gone, or fading as it may be, she was ready to get on her own two feet and try it alone. She'd tried to explain that to Matt but she didn't think he'd understood. He'd looked hurt and confused but, in typical Matt fashion, hadn't shown it. Instead, he'd quickly changed the subject and began talking about a recipe for rhubarb pie he'd found online.

At any rate, she was there now. In Shaker Town. Her suitcase unpacked, the toiletries and makeup from her carry-on bag littering the bathroom sink, and her laptop charging she grabbed Miss Dixie (her Nikon), threw on a light jacket, and stuck the room key in her pocket.

It was time to go exploring.

Upon checking in, she'd been met by the park curator, a tall

willowy man in his sixties by the name of Virgil Bailey. He proudly proclaimed he'd been at the park for more than thirty years; he'd started there as a demonstrator in the main building and could still make butter in a pinch. Although his pallor was gray and his hands thin and bony, the Ichabod Crane thing he had going on was offset by his jovial smile and warm eyes. The general manager was a vibrant brunette in her thirties. Just a year or two older than herself, she gave Taryn a hurried background of her museum qualifications, boasting that she'd first worked at neighboring White Hall State Historic Site in Madison County as curator and then moved up to Shaker Town the year before. "They needed someone young and fresh," she murmured, but stated it loudly enough so that Virgil heard her and shrugged.

Carol confessed that before taking the job she knew little about the Shakers. "You probably know more than I did when I started," she quipped as they strolled along the sidewalk to the site she'd be painting. "I read your dissertation on them. All I knew when I started here was that they were loud and couldn't have sex."

Well, that was one way of putting it.

"So what do you think *now*?" Taryn asked, genuinely interested in the young woman's take on a religious group she, herself, had been fascinated with since childhood.

Carol shrugged, her bobbed hair dancing in the breeze. "Pretty much the same thing. Oh, there's more to it, of course. They were hard workers, industrious, inventive people. Very passionate in a controlled kind of way. I would've been tempted to join them myself. But I wouldn't have," she added hastily. "I love my husband and kids too much."

"It is interesting that when whole families joined, if one of the members was to leave it was usually the woman," Taryn admitted. "You'd think it would be the man, unable to hack it without sex and intimacy but it was generally the women who couldn't stay."

"Probably because they couldn't take being separated from their children, you think?" Carol asked. "Because once they joined, their kids became kind of the group's kids and not their own anymore. And their male kids were taken from them altogether."

"I think that might be part of it," Taryn agreed. Of course, she didn't have children of her own but she could just imagine showing up and having her babies almost ripped from her arms, all in the name of God. The idea was horrifying on a primal level that Taryn didn't really understand.

The park was peaceful that early in the morning, an hour before the official opening time. The April sun was bright and cheerful and washed everything with a fresh cleanliness that made it difficult to remember the dingy, gray winter that had just recently passed over. Up ahead Taryn could hear the braying of the goats and sheep and off in a field a costumed man was hooking up a horse and wagon, getting them ready for the rides they'd give to tourists. A few stray chickens wandered into the road, saw the small group walking towards them, and tottered off again clucking their disapproval.

The park was kept exceptionally clean, organized, and well-maintained. Beautiful landscaping boasted flowers, perfectly groomed shrubbery, small gardens, and shade trees with comfortable benches parked under them along the path. The grass was evenly mowed, the fields freshly cut, and the trees perfectly trimmed. The Shakers would've kept it the same way in their day. They believed in keeping everything neat, tidy, and maintained. All belongings had a place, hence the pegs in the wall that kept everything from ladder-back chairs to dresses off the floor. They relied on built-ins when they could to keep their surface areas at a minimum. Their heavy furniture was well-made, solid, and plain and still coveted today. They'd perfected the straw broom design that could still be found in your local Target and Walmart. She was sure they would've appreciated the effort the park workers went to to keep up the appearance of the grounds today, although they might have been aghast at the tourists with their blue jeans, flip flops, and pajama bottoms. Taryn, for instance, was wearing a skirt that showed off her calves and a short-sleeved shirt that dipped low enough in the front to show the tiniest bit of cleavage. Scandalous.

"So here's where you'll mainly be working," Carol pointed as they came to a stop in a meadow. Here, there were three buildings in various states of repair. The largest was only one story, but the brick structure fanned out in a large rectangle and looked as though it had once held several rooms. The roof was

9

currently caved in on one side, the windows completely gone, and the entire left side of the building was flattened. It looked as though it had been burnt in a fire. Two smaller buildings flanked it, also brick, although the one to the right was barely more than a pile of rubble. The whole section was cordoned off with rope and the grass inside was thigh-high and unruly.

"Kind of an eyesore right now, huh?" Virgil chuckled, sticking his hands in his pockets.

"So tell me what I'm looking at," Taryn prodded. "Other than a few buildings."

Of course, they'd already told her what she would be painting when she took the job but now that she was seeing the site in person, she needed to hear it again.

"So that one in the middle," Carol pointed, "was the school. It was intact, up to about a year ago, and then lightning struck it. It's taken us this long to procure funding to get it fixed. Insurance would only cover so much. Even before it was destroyed, though, it was never historically accurate. It wasn't in much better shape when the state took over in the sixties and there wasn't a lot of research done to recreate it. So what we want is something that looks good and is accurate to the time period."

"That little 'un there to the right, it's never been fixed," Virgil pressed on. "It was a weaving building, a 'loom room,' if you will."

Taryn smiled as he raised his eyebrows at her and wagged them.

"We'd love to get it fixed and have a demonstrator in there with their loom, making things for the gift shop," Carol agreed. "We have one now, but she's in the main building. You know those looms take up a lot of space and she needs it. She needs somewhere she can spread out with everything. It would make an excellent addition to the park."

"And that other one?" Taryn asked.

"Just a dry house," Virgil shrugged. "Nothing much. But it's an eyesore and we might as well renovate. Getting it done would mean every single building on the grounds has been improved and is historically accurate. We'd be the only one in the country that has that."

"So we're talking recreating the buildings–"

"Inside and out," Carol interjected.

"Right. Inside and out. As well as the landscaping?" Taryn prodded.

"Yep," Virgil wagged his head emphatically. "We want to see the whole picture. Give the architect and landscaper something to work with and maybe even hang the painting up in the dining room. Use it for postcards even. The school was one of the most important parts of the place," he confided. "It's a pity it's in ruins."

"I'll do it," Taryn smiled. "And you can use it for your postcards, if you want. I have to say, too," she added with honesty, "that I am looking forward to this job more than anything else I've ever done. It's almost a dream come true."

Both Carol and Virgil nodded in unison–something they both apparently agreed upon. Taryn studied them now, standing in front of them with their backs to the sun. And she wondered if she was the only one who could all but smell the acrid scent of diabolical darkness that permeated the tranquil, well-maintained grounds and spring-fresh sky.

Now that she was alone and able to wander on her own accord,

Taryn had more time to gather her thoughts and explore. She'd been there before, of course, as well as to some of the other Shaker villages, but she was looking at it through different eyes this time, an artist's eyes. She wasn't researching the religious aspect of the order like she did for her dissertation or simply there to enjoy a weekend away (like she and Andrew had done a month before his fatal accident) but was there to work. Her paintings would be faithful reproductions of the original structures and these would help the architects and builders. They'd also be works of art to be reproduced and sold on a smaller scale. It was a big job and Taryn was honored to have won the bid for it. She'd worked hard at getting them to take her seriously, something that was becoming increasingly difficult thanks to the attention she was getting for her...forays with the paranormal. She'd Googled her name last week on a whim and wouldn't be doing that again—there had been more than fifty websites of forums and blogs all commenting on her supernatural skills with her camera and speculating her findings. It had really freaked her to be talked about in that manner—something she had no control over.

Now she was almost giddy at the thought of being able to live there for a month, working around the old buildings and history. Her heart thumping wildly in her chest, her belly fluttering—she was like a little kid at Christmas. This was her element. She'd babbled to Matt on the phone the night before, overcome with excitement at the thought of waking up every morning and being in a place she already loved. Matt had listened to her with patience, letting her ramble, but she knew the idea was lost on him. He wasn't a history person, had only indulged her all these years and been her chauffeur during their old-house expeditions because he adored her, and had no real understanding of what it was like to gaze upon a structure from the past and visualize the life it used to have. Although he could quote Star Wars, all six films, verbatim.

There were nearly forty buildings in all including a poultry house, laundry shop, tannery, dairy, barns, private dwellings and, of course, the meeting house. The dwellings and meeting house were perhaps the most important structures of all, at least as far as the tourists were concerned, and these were the first to be renovated. Before their renovations they'd served other purposes; for awhile the meeting house had been a mechanic's garage, something that made Taryn shudder. Those poor floors...

13

There were smaller dwellings, located on opposite sides of the village–one for the men and one for the women. They were tall, spacious structures with wide corridors and dormitory-style rooms. (Guests could also stay above the restaurant but she'd never been in those rooms.)

Around the "houses" were other buildings referred to as "shops." These were places where different activities were performed, such as basket-making, preserving, carpentry, laundry, and broom-making. Other structures at the park included several barns, a wood house, sawmill, and machinery shop for the brethren.

The meeting house, though sparkling white and sweet-looking, was simple both inside and out. The only significant defining characteristic was the two separate entrances on the front so that the men and women did not have to pass through the same door at the same time. They took their segregation seriously. Once inside, members of the order sat on opposite sides of the room, although during the services they were up moving around and allowed to sing and dance together. If they accidentally touched, which would've happened (you couldn't get three hundred people in there at once without some accidents) it was tolerated just as long as nobody made a habit of it.

The Shakers' worship services as a group revolved around their singing and dancing, which ranged from frenetic movements that looked wild and frenzied to childlike motions that bordered on the goofy. Sometimes their dancing was little more than a quiet shuffle. Other times, they would march and hold their hands out in front of them, pretending to gather something to their bodies. It was called "gathering a blessing" and they used it to bring positive energy to them.

They spent their time outside the meeting house serving the Creator through their hard work, cleanliness, and order.

The schoolhouse would be quaint and solid once renovations were complete. Although the Shakers didn't originally go for formal schooling, by the middle of the 1800's most settlements had added the schoolhouse and were intent on providing a quality education for their children. Some were even open to the public, although this one was not, at least as far as Taryn knew. It boasted two classrooms and was therefore not a traditional one-room school. She imagined that, due to the size, there were probably a couple of different teachers. Shakers were all pressed to find jobs at the settlement and work. In fact, hard work was what they were known for–after their erratic worshiping, of course. There weren't any idle hands or lazy days. Everything had a purpose, even the animals. No stray cats or dogs to keep as pets and love, just service animals that could work or provide food, wool, and leather. But the Shakers also tended to rotate jobs and move around, not staying in one position for long. They believed in equality and spreading their talents around, which was good if you hated a certain job but bad if you loved something and didn't get the chance to stay in it for long; they generally switched every month. She wasn't sure about the teachers, though. Perhaps they were full-timers. Men and women's jobs were considered equally important. The Shakers believed in gender equality before it was cool to do so.

Taryn couldn't help but smile as she walked around. The place was just so darn *peaceful.* Between the sunny daffodils, pastel dogwood trees, gently buzzing bees, and sounds of farm animals in the distance the village was alive with colors and noises that all but wiped away the modern world. She tried to ignore the shroud of bitterness that lurked somewhere in a layer above the park, all around her but nowhere to be seen. She'd not felt it on her other visits and was disappointed to find it now. She really *was* getting more sensitive, proof this "talent" of hers was going to follow her around for life.

The staff were all busy getting ready for the day ahead and barely paid notice to Taryn as she strolled down the paths, snapping pictures as she went. All dressed in period costumes and some in full character, Taryn felt as though she could've stepped back in time and been a visitor to the village, something the Shakers wouldn't have necessarily welcomed but wouldn't have been overtly rude about unless she overstepped her boundaries. She'd heard that on some days, the local townspeople would pack up picnic lunches, load their families up in the wagons, and find spots on the nearby hillsides where they could watch and listen to the foreign-sounding services that went on inside the meeting house. Between the raucous singing (no instruments since they believed nothing could improve upon the voice God gave you), hearty stomping, twirling on the wooden floors, and vibrant bouts of glossolalia must have made it the best show in town.

Taryn did not let the fact that she wasn't religious in the slightest bit dampen her interest in this spiritual group. She

16

might not have understood what they were up to, or understood the beliefs that were odd even for their time period, but she found it all endlessly fascinating.

The Ministry Shop was one of her favorite places, if for no other reason than she found the idea behind it interesting. The Ministry might have been the upper levels of the Shaker community but it didn't exempt them from working. They were supposed to do hard labor just as much as the brothers and sisters they oversaw, since they were all considered equal. The Ministry Shop was a special work space for the Elders and Eldresses, as a result. Taryn loved the pristine-white building with its cheerful facade and impeccable Shaker nod to cleanliness inside.

Other buildings at the park included the dairy shop (for the women), brethren's shop, laundry house, Trustee's Office, corn crib, carriage house, and tanyard.

A tall, thin man sat under a tree ahead of her, an open book in one hand and a Granny Smith in the other. He was gazing at the sky, however, and ignoring the pages and apple. As she drew nearer she could tell he was a park worker, thanks to his costume, but it fit him well and he looked at ease in it. He appeared to be around her age, thirty, although his face boasted some deep crinkles in his forehead and around his mouth–smile lines.

"Hi," he called with a smile when she was just a few feet away from him. "I was just taking a minute to enjoy the peace and quiet before the storm. You sneak in or something?"

She laughed and came to a stop. He was thin to the point of being bony and his face was pale, but there was a nice ruggedness to it that made her feel comfortable. He looked a little bit like a cowboy, like the Marlboro Man. "I just started working here," she explained.

"And they let you out without a dress? Or are you one of those progressive Shakers?" he teased.

"No, I'm an artist. I'm just here to paint," she laughed. "I'm Taryn."

"Dustin," he introduced himself as he rose to his feet and offered his hand. "I farm. My wife," he gestured vaguely in the direction of the meeting house, "is over there somewhere. She sings and works with the music. Does some herb lore on the side."

"That must be nice, working together like this," Taryn said appreciatively, quickly remembering all the jobs she and her deceased husband, Andrew, had worked on together. She'd enjoyed being in his presence throughout the day, even though they didn't do the same thing. He was an architect, she an artist. But simply being on the same job site and knowing the other was near was comforting. They genuinely liked each other and liked being in each other's company.

And then he died, that damnable Camaro.

"It is nice," he agreed. "Nice to not have to eat lunch by yourself. Lydia, she's my wife, has been here almost ten years. This is my sixth."

"So you're old pros," Taryn smiled. "I might have to hit you up when I need some intel."

18

"Be happy to oblige," he promised. A small beep emitted from a watch deep in a vest pocket and he patted it, quieting the noise. "And that's my alarm. Means I have to get to the shop now. Come find me and Lydia later. We'll show you the ropes, she'll give you the female gossip. You know, the good stuff."

Taryn was still smiling as he walked off, a casual saunter in the dappled shade of the trees. Off in the distance a young woman raised her arm and waved at him and he blew her a kiss. She pretended to catch it and put it in her pocket. Taryn felt a little pang then, but it was a blissful one. She had *good* feelings about this job. It was a gorgeous location, a different kind of work environment, and she might have even just made herself a friend. Lord knew that didn't happen often. And if there *were* ghosts around, well, they *had* to be friendly ones. After all, it wasn't like Shaker Town had ever been a place of murder, crime, and corruption.

CHAPTER 2

"So, how did the first day on the job go?" Matt asked.

She'd raced back to her room after her exploration, excited to get him on the phone. She was damn set on doing this job alone, to prove she could handle whatever came with it, but it didn't mean she didn't want to share her day and news. She also knew Matt was waiting patiently by the phone, waiting for her call. It was her habit of giving him a rundown on the first day of any new job, just as it was his job to patiently let her talk and use words like "buttresses" and "wainscoting" and pretend he knew what the hell she was talking about.

She had him on speaker phone while she lounged on the firm, but comfortable, bed in her room. An episode of *Friends* was on, was muted in the background. She couldn't hear it but the colors and movements made her feel less lonely. Matt had just gotten home from work and was puttering around his place, probably getting something together for dinner. He loved cooking more than anyone else she knew. He loved the organization, the instructions, the ability to experiment in a controlled environment—he even liked the tidiness of the cleanup. She felt a little pang for him, for the order he brought to her often-frazzled lifestyle, and grinned.

"Good I think," she answered carefully. She'd been ignoring the tense feeling that tugged at her all day, trying to pass it off as first-day-on-the-job jitters. After all, everything had gone perfectly fine and she was happy to be there. The people were all friendly and likable so far. She had nothing to worry about and wasn't going to worry Matt with some misgivings she wasn't even able to articulate yet. "I just explored today, sat in on some demonstrations and talks. Went into all the buildings. Learned to make a basket. It was fun."

She took in her lopsided basket now, drying on a towel on the bureau, with pride. A young, pretty woman with long dark hair and a name tag that read "Heather" had been patient enough to go over all the steps at least three times with her. It wouldn't win her any awards, but she liked making practical stuff. Taryn figured she could store her makeup in it.

"Sounds good," Matt murmured absently, making her wonder if he'd even heard a word she said. And then, "Ooh! I learned a better way to make poached eggs this afternoon. Apparently, if you swirl the water a little bit first..."

Matt proceeded to go off on a lecture about perfecting not only the poached egg but hollandaise sauce. (He might have been an astro engineer but he'd definitely missed his calling as a television chef on a cooking show.) Taryn let him ramble, unperturbed. She used the opportunity as s chance to hear his voice and paint her toenails at the same time.

He humored her when it came to her own work and love of history but Matt himself had little use for art or the past. He was fixated on the future, on what adventures the world could offer now, thanks to modern technology and other innovations. Both often felt they were born in the wrong time periods–but several hundred years apart. Still, they managed to make it work and their relationship was the longest one Taryn had known, especially now that both her parents and grandmother were long passed on.

Taryn waited until his excitement slowed down (the boy really *could* get worked up over Teflon) and came to a pause in his speech before gently changing the subject. "So do you think you'll be able to make it up here in a few weeks?" They hadn't seen each other in almost a month– the longest they'd been apart since starting this new chapter in their relationship.

Both were proceeding a little cautiously with their new developments, still feeling the other out. They were as good of friends as they'd ever been, but once they'd introduced sex into the picture the ballgame had gotten a lot more interesting. Taryn thought she'd have trouble being naked with a guy who'd once wailed tears of pain after he fell off his bike and landed on the sidewalk in front of half the school. (She still remembered

22

helping him to her house, cleaning the dirt out of his "wound" and applying a Fraggle Rock Band-Aid to his dark skin.) Turned out, nakedness or any of the other stuff wasn't as weird as she'd imagined. It was actually pretty good. The part of his personality that was rigid and controlled in the rest of the world knew how to let loose when it needed to. But still...neither knew where they were headed and it made them both nervous.

Matt sighed, irritation on his breath, and considered their distance. "I don't know. I planned on it, but we have a bunch of things to clear off the table down here. I'm going to try."

Taryn was disappointed, but couldn't push him, of course. He'd taken off almost two months to spend with her in Georgia in the fall, and he'd almost been killed there, so she didn't blame him for not jumping at the bit to get involved in more of her drama. Besides, she didn't want to be the damsel in distress again. Whatever was happening to her, health-wise and ghost-wise, was for her to deal with. He'd come to her rescue over and over again, almost with more obligation than feeling, and it bothered her. It was time that she learned to maneuver her own life.

That didn't mean she didn't want to see him. She was human; she got lonely. He was, after all, her best friend.

"Do you think you could come down here?" he asked hopefully.

Taryn struggled not to become annoyed. After all, she had just asked him the same thing. Still, historically she'd done the traveling to get to him and sometimes she felt just shy of stalking. "I just started this job. I don't know if I can leave it. I'll see how it goes, though."

Matt sighed and even in the small noise she could hear disappointment. "So tell me about the Shakers a little," he suggested. "What did they believe in? Who started them?"

This was something Taryn could talk about with ease. After all, she'd studied them in college. "Well, think of them like a communist cult, only in a good way," she began.

Matt laughed, a nice rich sound that flooded through the phone. She felt better. "Okay."

"Seriously. They believed in communal living, confessing their sins, separating themselves from the rest of the world....oh, and celibacy."

"How'd they get away with that?"

"They didn't, really," Taryn answered. "It's why they all died out."

"Geeze. And they were into the religious experiences, seeing things, talking to God–those things?"

"Yes. Ann Lee, the woman who founded them, was very charismatic. The Shakers thought she embodied the second coming of the Christ spirit as manifested on Earth."

"Huh."

"I have my own theories about her. It has to do with her losing all her children and being in a weird marriage. But I don't want to get into that."

Now they were both silent, either lost in thought or with little else to say. Taryn went ahead and wrapped up the conversation with a hurried "love you" (saying that always made her uncomfortable; she couldn't help it) and hung up. Feeling slightly depressed now, she bunched up the feather pillow and un-muted the television.

It was growing dark outside and she'd already had supper in the restaurant. She needed to drive into Harrodsburg, the neighboring town, and stock up on snacks but she was too lazy to move. In Georgia a doctor had finally put all the symptoms that had been plaguing her for years together and diagnosed her with Ehlers-Danlos Syndrome, a connective tissue disorder. On the plus side, it made her freakishly flexible and she could do "tricks" that both amazed and repulsed people. On the down side, it caused a whole host of problems that started with her head and went all the way down to her toes. It was responsible for her chronic pain (bursitis, tendinitis, osteoarthritis, scoliosis, hundreds of micro tears all over her body and a labral tear in her left hip) and fatigue—making her relieved she wasn't as lazy as she'd thought. (Well, she still was, but *now* she had an excuse.)

When she returned to Nashville and saw the geneticist at Vanderbilt she'd been further diagnosed with crossover symptoms of Vascular Ehlers-Danlos Syndrome, a more serious form, and that was causing its own set of problems. She didn't have the genetic components to make it true VEDS, but still had worrying symptoms. Taryn had an aortic aneurysm they were keeping an eye on and varicose veins that were ugly more than anything else. She'd lost her appendix and spleen after Christmas due to ruptures. Her maternal grandmother had died of an arterial rupture in her sleep but she'd been in her eighties.

25

Taryn still had a lot of living left to do. But she could do it tomorrow.

In the meantime, she might as well enjoy some downtime before the real work started.

The cries woke her up. Deep and ragged, they were instantly recognizable to her; only someone who had experienced that much grief themselves knew them for what they were. She sat straight up in bed, the pillow under her dropping to the hardwood floor with a light "thump." The room was coal black and she belatedly realized the television must have been set on a timer, going off in the middle of the night. She hated to be in a dark, quiet room alone.

Her heart pounding, she listened with curiosity to the uncontrollable sobs that sounded neither male nor female and her heart ached. Was it someone in another room? She didn't think so; as far as she knew she was the only one staying in that particular building. Someone outside then?

Quietly, Taryn slipped out of bed and tiptoed across the floor in her bare feet, the wood cold against her skin. The lacy curtains were a flimsy barrier between her and the night sky and before she'd even pushed them aside she could see the pale figure below, alone on the grass. It was a woman then, a slender woman of undecipherable age. Her long dark hair billowed out behind her, whipped by the wind, her white nightgown a contrast to the dark sky. Despite the security lamp above her, no shadow followed her on the ground.

At first, the woman was motionless, only her sobs a testament to her presence. She could've been a statue, a pale tree swaying in the wind. But then, as her cries grew louder and swirled up towards Taryn, carried by the breeze, she began to sprint across the grounds. Taryn watched as she ran towards the old stone fence that surrounded the building and then gasped in surprise as she ran *through* it. The figure disappeared then; as suddenly as she'd materialized she was gone.

With a leap back from the window, Taryn placed her hand on her chest, as if to manually steady her heartbeat. A ghost then, she thought, as the chills ran up her arms. The hairs on her head stood at attention. It would make sense that the grounds were haunted, if for no other reason than their age and the former spiritual nature of the compound. Just because there was a ghost, though, didn't mean *she* had to do anything about it, she reminded herself.

But as she climbed back into bed and flipped on the lamp for comfort, she shivered in dread and pulled the blanket around her like a shroud. She would *have* to do something about it. Because just before the figure passed through the fence like a puff of smoke she'd turned towards Taryn's window and gazed right at her. The two had made contact.

Game on.

Creating the outside of the buildings would not be as much of

an issue as the interiors. There were still several Shaker school buildings still standing around the country, not to mention loads of examples of schools from that time period and areas that were *not* Shaker-affiliated. The dry house would be a cinch (there wasn't much to it structurally to recreate, even though it was mostly gone) and the weaving building wasn't as deteriorated as it had appeared on first inspection. The interiors, however, would be trickier. Shaker style had its own nuances and definitive elements; it was still emulated today. If she screwed something up then even laypeople would notice; she wouldn't be able to get as creative as she liked.

Normally, Taryn would begin the job by doing some charcoal sketches. She was going to approach this one a little differently, however, and start with some research. (To be honest, she wasn't entirely sure what a "dry house" was; she'd just nodded her head and smiled at Virgil when he showed it to her.) Luckily, the park had an archives and research room that she was given free reign of (within reason, of course; she couldn't take anything out of it) and she intended to use it to her advantage.

So, on her first full day at Shaker Town Taryn found herself locked in a good-sized room, alone, surrounded by piles of dusty ledgers, drawings, letters, and books. She learned about Shaker furniture, Shaker inventions (a Shaker woman actually invented the circular saw-fascinating), Shaker clothing (plain and same was the theme), and Shaker design. By lunch she'd been studying for almost four and a half hours and felt like she was back in school again. She'd barely touched the tip of the iceberg even after all that time. The Shakers were excellent record keepers.

Still, her tummy rumbled and she was no fool. Taryn knew when it was time to eat and since the park provided her meals she let herself out of the room, making sure to lock it behind her, and made her way to the restaurant.

The beautiful dining room with the glorious winding, circular staircase (featured prominently in all the brochures) was crowded, probably thanks to the gorgeous weather they were having. Young, yuppifying women with screeching toddlers fighting spoons in high chairs and relaxed-looking retirees clinked glasses of teas, slathered real butter on rolls, and oohed over dessert trays. The dinner crowd had been somewhat different the night before, a little more reserved maybe. She tried to imagine living in the area and being a stay-at-home mom, loading the kids up in the Suburban and taking them to spend a day at the park, complete with horse and wagon ride and a trip down the river on the old-fashioned sightseeing boat. It sounded kind of nice.

Taryn, deciding that if she didn't start watching her weight now she'd weigh a ton by the time she left, chose a nice spring salad and bowl of tomato bisque soup. She was still passing on the sweet tea, thanks to her stint at Windwood Farm, and hadn't quite gotten around to giving up Coke–her main vice. While she waited for her food she thumbed through a well-worn Peter Straub novel she'd stuck in her day pack and set out to enjoy her lunch.

She was still feeling a little high at the idea of actually being there. In college she'd been a tour guide at a historical home in Nashville and had always wondered what it might have been like to work there at Shaker Town. She still felt kindred spirits with other costumed guides whenever she visited a park like the one she was at now and made a terrible guest herself, always wanting to take over the tours and lecture herself. Staying there in the beautifully appointed, but simple, rooms and eating glorious meals for a month was almost like being at a resort. Granted, a resort where the women wore bonnets and long-sleeved dresses and there was a bit more blacksmithing than usual...

Her server was a plump middle-aged woman with shockingly red hair, bright green eyes, and the faint shadow of a mustache on her upper lip. Though a little on the homely side, her personality and cheerfulness were so contagious that Taryn instantly forgot her physical attributes. "That all you want to eat," she demanded, setting Taryn's soup down in front of her.

"Well, and the salad," Taryn laughed. "There's a little more coming, right?"

30

"It's good, but it ain't enough to feed a grasshopper," she snorted. Her name tag read "Ellen" and Taryn estimated her to be in her early fifties.

"I'm going to be here awhile. If I don't pace myself I'll gain fifty pounds," Taryn explained.

"Oh yeah, you're the painter. Well, I'll be here at supper, too. Sit here when you come back and I'll load you up with some bread and fruit for you to take back to your room. It's not like you can make a midnight run to Taco Bell once we close down the kitchen. I mean, you *can*," she mused, "but it's a long run for the border."

It was true; the park was kind of out in the middle of nowhere. Taryn liked that but it did make it hard to pop out to the store when you had a craving.

"Thanks," she replied. "I appreciate it. I got the munchies last night."

"Girl, I live for the munchies. My purse is a regular 7/11."

Taryn spent the rest of the afternoon holed back up in the

research room, her fingers blackening from the grimy pages and the bright sunlight muted by the heavy drapes meant to keep the books and other important documents from fading. The reading was enlightening and she could've kept it up for weeks, but she was really there to search for inspiration for the buildings so she had to skip over a lot of information that didn't pertain to her current job.

Pity, though. She loved reading about the Shakers' regimented lives and their complete control over daily living, doctrines, and rules. They might not have believed in procreating, but they were far ahead of their time when it came to women's rights and racial issues. Women held the highest positions and, indeed, it was a woman who started the Shaker movement–Mother Ann, she was called, although she didn't ever live at Pleasant Hill.

The Shakers grew by taking in orphans or other unwanted children and by recruiting those of a like-minded mindset. The Elders would sit on the second floor of the meeting house during services, gazing down at everyone from tiny windows. From there, they'd check out the other onlookers (visitors were allowed to come watch the meetings although they still had to be segregated with men on one side and women on the other). Afterwards, if they'd seen someone they thought they might be able to hook, they'd seek them, ninja-style, and talk the place up.

Okay, maybe not exactly like that, but it's the way Taryn saw things in her mind.

In the beginning, when Kentucky was still the "wild west," times were hard in the area. Rough winters meant cold weather and sometimes a shortage of food. The Shakers offered sturdy buildings, beds, hot meals, and heat. Recruitment was easier then. Everyone wanted to be a Shaker!

The idea of celibacy was a lot easier to stomach when your belly was empty and your joints aching from the snow and wind. But then, as the warm weather came and game once again became plentiful, gardens sprouting, nature called in other ways and suddenly the strict rules became overbearing. Those who had joined for less than honorable intentions found themselves packing up and leaving and heading back home. These were often referred to as "winter Shakers" for their fickle ways. Of course, while they might be welcomed back once more when the winter came again, it wouldn't always be open arms that reached for them.

When Taryn was finished with her research for the afternoon she took another walk along the pathways, stopping at the meeting house when she heard singing drifting through the open door. Visitors were seated on hard, wooden benches inside, facing a large man who walked down a large aisle, raising his voice so that it reverberated off the walls. The song was about simplicity, freedom, and living a life without frills. His voice was strong and powerful and the audience watched in rapture; even the small children gazed at him with something between fear and enchantment.

Taryn slipped into the room and parked herself next to a family of four, the bench uncomfortable under her, reminding her she'd missed a dose of her pain medication. It was probably psychological, but since getting the Ehlers-Danlos Syndrome diagnosis she was almost certain the pain in her hips and legs had intensified. As she let herself fall into the music and rhythm of the singer's staccato steps back and forth across the large room, however, she was able to temporarily forget about the pain and lose herself in her thoughts.

Some people were under the false impression that the Shakers' erratic singing and dancing was unstructured, as freestyle as the Pentecostals whose services sometimes resembled epileptic fits. If you'd never seen glossolalia then you were in for a surprise; talking in tongues could be as creepy as anything in a horror movie. They weren't unstructured, though. Though they did use their glossolalia, singing, and dancing to encourage religious experiences and communicate with the heavenly father, the songs were chosen in advance, the dance steps pre-determined, and the service as regimented as anything else they did. Having that religious experience was important–so much so that some of the leaders thought there was something wrong if at least one person didn't get the spirit in them and react. The next service might be longer, more involved. One meeting lasted for more than twenty-four hours. Taryn thought if she'd been there for that one she'd have been faking a little spirit talk, if for no other reason than to eat.

Taryn, an avid music lover, reveled in the sound of the deep baritone filling the walls built for such entertainment. Even with the doors open at either end, the acoustics were extraordinary and she found herself closing her eyes, leaning back on her hands, and enjoying the vocalization. The people surrounding her were quiet, respectfully listening to the songs as they rang out one after another.

Then, sensing an end, Taryn opened her eyes and took out her camera, Miss Dixie. She zoomed in on the singer, scanned the captivated audience, and then took a wide angle shot to encompass the room's entirety. Her memory card would be full soon at this rate; she'd already taken a ton of photos.

Grinning and with a light heart, when the show was over Taryn stood up with the rest of the crowd and made her way out the door, unintentionally walking through the women's side.

Much, much later, after stuffing herself with pork roast and

pecan pie, Taryn relaxed in her room, her red flannel nightgown pulled down to her feet to keep the chill off. She was having a hard time staying warm, despite having the heat on, and flannel was her friend. She hoarded her flannel nightgowns the same way some women did expensive lingerie.

An aimless reality show was on for background noise as she flipped through her photos on her laptop. Her New Year's resolution was to edit her photos as she went along rather than waiting until the very end and trying to do it all at once. She had thousands of photos to do something with and was afraid she'd never get around to it. Something always came up.

Taryn smiled as she cropped and fixed images of the horses leading the wagons, the goats in the barn, the oxen in the field... She'd caught a particularly charming shot of a toddler leaning forward into a clump of daffodils, the delight on her little face enough to make Taryn tear up.

The images of her lunch and dinner, food porn at its best, made her stomach grumble and she vowed to head into town the next day and pick up some snacks to hoard in her room.

She hadn't taken any interior shots except for those at the meeting house. She'd spent so much time in the research room and walking around outside that she hadn't explored the insides.

Feeling the urge to go to the bathroom coming on, she was halfway off the bed when the image on the screen grabbed her and brought her fumbling back, nearly losing her balance and toppling to the floor.

The costumed performer stood in the center of the floor, his eyes closed and mouth open as he lost himself in song. The audience gazed at him, wonder and rapture on their faces. His portly stomach burst from his period-style pants and his hands were clasped behind his back, just as they'd been in real life. At first, nothing looked off about the photograph. But on second glance there behind him, where there hadn't been anyone before, was the lone silhouette of a woman. Her hands were raised in the air, open to Heaven, her skirt twirled around her as she spun on the sunlit floors. A ribbon on her bonnet had come loose and was soaring through the air, hovering several feet from the ground. The pale blue of the fabric almost white as a ray of sunlight hit it.

The image was as plain as day, her features distinct. The fact that she hadn't been there at all that afternoon and that Taryn was able to see right through her were the only clues that she was a ghost.

CHAPTER 3

*O*ne of Taryn's favorite parts of the day was when,

while getting dressed in the late morning, the sounds of Dustin's wife Lydia doing the first musical show drifted down the tree-lined path that ran through the heart of the park and filled her room. Thanks to the meeting house's glorious acoustics Lydia's voice, which would've sounded like an angel's under ordinary circumstances, was magnificent under the high ceilings. It resounded through the walls and shot outside where each beautiful note wrapped around every leaf, through every tree limb, and even filtered through the windows of the other buildings so that visitors would stop, listen, and hold their breaths until she finished.

Taryn generally liked to sleep in and considered anything before noon as "early." Her work allowed her to set her own hours, but the early morning sun and late afternoon rays were truly the best lights to work with. Of course. The Shakers had risen at 4:30 am in the summer time and only slightly later in the winter; it would've been dark when they got up regardless. Sometimes Taryn was just going to bed at that time.

At the first few notes, Taryn crawled out of bed, threw on her thick white bathrobe, and wandered over to the window where she leaned against the glass and gazed at the undisturbed meadow. It was empty now, freshly mowed, and peaceful. Difficult to believe just a few nights before Taryn had watched the ghost woman all but dance through it and disappear. Although Lydia and the meeting house were a good ten-minute walk from her lodgings, Taryn could hear her as plainly as if she were in the next room, the sounds of the Shaker anthem, "Simple Gifts," grabbing hold of her heart and squeezing just a little.

It had been a long time since Taryn had painted multiple buildings and she wanted to make sure she did it well. Everyone from the tourism board to the guests and governor himself would be seeing her paintings, and probably scrutinizing them, and she didn't want to let anyone down.

Of course, staying there at Shaker Town was more of a vacation than anything, if she was totally honest with herself. People traveled from all over the state to eat in the famous restaurant that served vegetables grown right there on the site, to sleep in the comfortable Shaker-style beds in the renovated buildings, and to see the craft demonstrations. They boasted many events throughout the year including a fund-raising bike trek, ghost tours, candlelight tours, concerts, and more. She was lucky that not only did she get to be there for free—*they* were paying *her*.

Taryn was enjoying this time of year, when everything felt, looked, and tasted fresh and clean. Although it was cool in the mornings all the way up until noon and she had to wear long sleeves and a jacket to stand outside at her easel, as the day wore on she was able to shed these and enjoy the warm sunshine on her back. The daffodils had popped up with the irises and grew around the fence posts and in clusters in the meadows.

On slow days when there were only a few stragglers or elder hostel groups following brightly-colored umbrellas she liked to close her eyes and imagine she had the place to herself. She could hear the bees buzzing around the blossoms, hear the faint rumble of airplanes high in the sky, and catch the calls of the horses and cows out in the field—and that was it. After a few months of turmoil, stress, and dealing with the aftermath of what happened in Georgia (including having to give testimony at a stressful but mercifully short trial) she was glad for the peace.

Unlike other places where she'd worked, the employees there at Shaker Town seemed to genuinely like what they were doing and enjoyed being there. She'd hung out with some of them while they were on their break and so far she'd only heard the normal complaints—aching feet, unruly kids, sore throats from talking so much, etc. She'd been a tour guide at a historical home in Nashville during her college years so she could sympathize with all those things. But, unlike the situations at her previous place of employment, she didn't hear these guys complaining about small pay scale, demanding and unreasonable bosses, uncomfortable costumes, and lack of respect. So that had to be saying something. The only main complaint she had was that the closest business for her to make

41

a mad chocolate dash to or rent Redbox from was a ten minute drive away in the small hamlet of Burgin.

The day was over for the employees yet some were still

lingering, trying to unwind before driving back to Harrodsburg, Perryville, Danville, or Lexington. Taryn had originally been lying alone on her quilt by the pond, reading a book, but was soon joined by Dustin and his wife Lydia, George who worked maintenance, and Julie–resident bartender. Since it was a Friday night they'd be having happy hour out on the patio soon, along with live music, so Julie was resting before she started setting up. Taryn had only met the petite, tanned MA student once before but liked her bubbly, youthful personality. Taryn was prone to silence, enjoying solitude to the point of it being a flaw, so surrounding herself with others who were more outgoing was sometimes necessary. George was a middle-aged man originally from Delaware, a state Taryn sometimes totally forgot even existed. The only thing she knew about it was that she occasionally got collection notices from credit cards with it as the return address.

"Long day today," Dustin sighed, leaning back on his forearms and gazing at the sparkling water before them. Lydia nodded, taking care with her voice. Despite the great acoustics, the sheer amount of talking she had do to throughout the day left her throat raw.

"I'll say," George grunted, tossing a rock into the water and watching it make small ripples.

Taryn hadn't made up her mind about George yet. He was built like a truck–solid and strong with broad shoulders and the longest arms she'd ever seen. He seemed friendly enough but had a perpetual scowl on his face and she couldn't tell if he was angry or just had a natural resting bitch face.

"Hey, at least you guys can go home now," Julie grumbled. "My day's just getting started."

Lydia patted the younger girl's arm in sympathy and then laid her head over on Dustin's lap. Lydia was pretty in a hardened way. Her hair, though tucked in a neat little bun, was dry and brittle from too many colorings and perms. (To be honest, though, considering what they all put their hair through in the 1980s they were lucky any of them had any left. Taryn shuddered at her old routine which consisted of holding one side out with a large pick, vigorously spraying it with Aqua Net, and then blow drying it until her head burned...all in the name of creating "wings.") Lydia had the skin of a smoker but her eyes were bright green and sparkled when they landed on her husband.

"You get a fun job, though," Dustin teased her. "You get to pour the booze."

"Dude, drunks at Shaker Town are still drunks," Julie lamented and they all laughed.

43

Being with these folks, who were much closer to her age, was a far cry from being around the kids she'd met in Georgia. Taryn had been sucked into that world, allured by the attention and youthful energy that made her feel alive and excited. She hadn't had many friends in high school (just Matt, really) and the temptation to hang out with a group who wanted to have fun and hung onto her words was tantalizing, even if they were much younger than her. These guys, however, had all graduated from college, been in the workforce for awhile, and had real lives. They made her nervous since she'd always had trouble talking to people her own age, but she was trying to fit in with them. It was her loneliness that had gotten her into more than one scrape in the past.

"I, for one, didn't think this day would ever end," Dustin moaned. He slipped off his shoes and Lydia's head shot up from his lap. While she pretended to gag and choke, everyone laughed.

"A little warning next time there buddy," she sputtered.

"Sorry. Feet hurt," he shrugged. "I must have been on the plant tour today because I swear every single person who came over to the farm just wanted to know what all the plants were."

"I have everyone beat," George grumbled. "Between the horse shit, the oxen shit, and the kid vomit I cleaned up today I could fertilize the whole south field."

"You need signs," Lydia pointed out to Dustin. "And George, you need a new job. Not enough money in the world...But if Dustin was hosting the vegetation tour then I must have been hosting the haunted one."

44

Taryn, hearing her calling, perked up. "Yeah? You telling ghost stories? What did they want to know?"

"The usual," Lydia shrugged. "Which buildings are haunted, has anyone been murdered here, have I ever seen a ghost? Etcetera, etcetera."

"It's all stupid rumors," George said, rolling his eyes. "I've been here five years and never seen a thing. Nothing that's scarier than a kid throwing a temper tantrum, that is."

"Any place that's been around this long, there are going to be ghosts," Lydia retorted. "I've never *seen* anything, but I've heard some stuff."

"I saw something once," Julie shrugged. "I *think* I did anyway. After the kitchen closed down one night and we'd brought everything back in from the patio. I was carrying the cups back inside and saw a woman kind of, I don't know, dancing I guess you'd say. In the road."

"Couldn't it have been a guest?"

"I thought so at first," Julie said hesitantly. "But then....Oh, you all are going to laugh at me!"

"Probably. But tell us anyway," George prodded, interested in spite of himself.

"You could see through her. It was only for a second or two and then she disappeared." Julie's face was bright red, embarrassment flooding over her. Taryn could understand that. She also grew embarrassed talking about her experiences–and many of them were now well-documented for posterity's sake.

"I'm staying over there in the north forty in one of the shops," Taryn added. "That building meant to be haunted?"

"We don't want to scare you," Lydia chided, frowning slightly at Julie.

"Oh good," Taryn smiled. "Then you clearly haven't heard of me or what I do. That's refreshing."

"Are you a ghost hunter?" Dustin asked, intrigued. "You can't say something like that and not share."

Taryn felt her face blush. She really *hadn't* been trying to open that door. "We'll talk later. I'll save all the gory details for another day. But seriously...any stories I should know about?"

Lydia shrugged. "Well, you know. People did die here. Old age, sickness, suicide."

"Shhh!" Dustin warned. "You know we're not supposed to admit there was discourse amongst the Shakers!"

"Just one murder and it was a long time ago," George said, breaking up the laughter. "I don't think the killer is still out there. He'd be more than one hundred fifty years old."

"What happened?" Taryn asked.

"Oh, God, it was awful," Julie shuddered. "Got whacked to death or something. Nobody knows. But the story is that he was found in pieces all over the park–an arm here, a leg there...And a big pool of blood in the–"

"Julie!" Lydia hissed.

"What?" Taryn asked, looking from one woman to the other.

"She doesn't want me to tell you that there was a big pool of blood in the bottom floor of your building," Julie replied smugly. "They couldn't get it up. Been there, like George said, forever. Finally just replaced the wood."

"Good Lord," Taryn said, leaning back on her forearms. "So am I going to wake up to some guy wandering around my room, trying to find his head?"

They all laughed, breaking a slightly tense mood, and the subject was changed. As Taryn walked back to her room, however, the padding of tennis shoes hitting the sidewalk came up behind her and made her slow down. It certainly wasn't a ghost, unless the ghost wore Nike's.

"Hey," Julie called. She was winded and Taryn realized she'd been running after her. "I know who you are and what you do. I Googled you on my phone after you left."

"Yeah?" Taryn smiled nervously.

"It's okay. I believe in ghosts. And to answer your question, there are a lot of stories about this place. *A lot.* Guests stay here all the time and report things. And I think the old cemetery is pretty creepy myself. But the woman I saw? I'm *not* the only one. She seems harmless enough, but that wasn't the first time I saw her. Or the last."

"Who is she?"

Julie shrugged. "Don't know. I'm guessing she died young here, though. Maybe she got sick. Or something. There's some books about the Shakers and the ghosts but nothing like her."

Taryn assented, chewing on her bottom lip. "If I hear or see or learn anything, I'll let you know."

"Awesome sauce," Julie laughed. "Well, I have to go mix drinks. Come down later if you want. Happy hour will start soon!"

Taryn was left standing alone on the sidewalk, just the sound of the bees buzzing in a hive on one of the buildings filling the air. *They need to remove that,* Taryn thought absently. *Someone is going to get hurt.*

CHAPTER 4

*T*he sun was beating down on her legs, the rough

linen of her dress pulled up to her knees to allow the rays more
access. They were reddening, and she'd pay for it later if they
burned, but for now she enjoyed the luxury of the warmth. The

feel of the sun above her and soft grass under her lulled her into a dreamworld, a place where she was only a small part of the world around her.

Suddenly, the world was blocked out by a shadow above her. The darkness spread over her, blanketing her with its sudden coolness. She looked up, startled, but smiled primly and covered her legs with her hem.

The man smiling back at her had large, brown eyes and dark hair with just a hint of auburn. His straw hat shaded his face but she knew it well enough.

As he squatted down next to her his britches, beaten soft from too many washings, brushed against her hand. The feeling of being so close to him, of touching him, sent hot lightning bolts coursing through her arms and legs until they settled into a not-unpleasant knot in her belly.

Neither spoke but remained together in silence, the sounds of the outside world forgotten. There was content unlike anything she'd ever known, the peace of knowing she was exactly where she was meant to be. It was that perfect moment she'd always dreamed about, read about before arriving, and she longed to grasp it, put it in a little box, and carry it with her everywhere she went.

Then, he reached over and plucked a long stray blade of grass from her face, grazing her cheek with the pad of his thumb. She lifted her hand to touch him, he was just inches away, but he was descending quickly into an invisible hole; tumbling farther and farther from her reach until all she could do was scream out his name.

Taryn was a sweater when her nerves got to her and nothing set her off like a bad dream. Although nothing bad technically happened in her sleep, the feeling of reaching out to the man and being unable to gasp him bothered her more than a legion of zombies or vampires. She woke drenched with sweat. A sniff under her arms told her she didn't stink but she'd still need a shower, and her heart was pounding. Her duvet and pillow were wet and cold as well. They'd need to be washed so Taryn stripped them off and placed them outside her door for housekeeping.

She chewed on the images of the man slipping from her grasp all morning until, at last, she took a break with her sketching and called Matt.

"I had a bad dream last night," she complained, feeling like a little kid running to her parents' bed. (Well, perhaps not *her* parents' bed, but a normal one. Her parents would've shooed her out and sent her back, scientific explanation for bad dreams in hand.)

"Yeah, what was it?" Matt was at work now, as she knew he'd be, and she could hear the quiet tapping on his keyboard. She must have caught him in the middle of something. He was distracted and, of course, she was keeping him from something.

"Oh, nothing I guess," she replied, feeling silly. "Probably just my overactive imagination here at the village. Combined with too many romance novels."

"Yeah? What about?" he asked, not realizing he'd already asked that question. He really *must* be distracted, she thought.

"Nothing," Taryn assured him. "I'll call you back sometime after dinner."

"Okay!" he called cheerfully.

Taryn stuffed the phone back in her pocket and looked down the gravel road. The stones had picked up a cloud of dust, covering her brown Walmart sandals in white powder. She didn't know where she was heading; she just knew she needed a walk. There were already a few tourists out and she smiled as a young mother walked by, holding the hands of a five-year-old boy and toddler girl. The little girl was barefoot and Taryn had no idea how she was able to walk comfortably over the rocks. They looked happy, though, and it made something inside of her melt just a little.

Was her biological clock starting to tick? Maybe. Her doctor back in Nashville had told her that pregnancy would be difficult with Ehlers-Danlos Syndrome, that she might experience more muscular and joint pain than normal as the pregnancy hormones kicked in and her weight increased. And then there was a chance of uterine rupture or placenta problems. Pre-term labor and other things that made her shudder.

But Taryn liked kids and if she wanted to have them she wouldn't let health issues get in the way. She wasn't sure she liked the idea of her kids inheriting something painful and as symptomatic as her EDS was, especially from her, but Taryn was realistic enough to know that in this day and age everyone was bound to end up with something anyway.

She just wasn't sure she was ready to have any. She and Matt had barely talked about the future. She still wasn't even sure she could call what they were doing "dating." At the moment it wasn't any different than what they'd been doing since they were kids, only they were having sex now. And she wasn't doing it with anyone else.

The gravel road ran past the old stone shop, carpenter's shop, and west family dwelling then rounded a small bend. She hadn't realized she'd walked so far and was about to turn around when something up ahead on the left past the corn crib caught her eye; she'd found the old cemetery Julie spoke of.

With Miss Dixie slung around her neck she proceeded, intent on checking it out. Taryn loved cemeteries; she always thought of them as safe places and especially loved the old ones with their crumbling stones sticking haphazardly from the ground and ancient wrought-iron fences.

This one, positioned on a little hill overlooking the valley, didn't have nearly as many stones as she would have expected. There were perhaps a dozen or so and the dates stopped after the turn of the century. Maybe, she thought, family members who lived on the outside had taken their loved ones away to bury them. Or maybe there was another, newer, one on the other side of the park. She needed to dig out her map again.

She could hear the sounds of the cars whizzing by on the main road below her, and somewhere off in the distance was the vague chatter of school children on a field trip, but she had the cemetery to herself. No other tourists had made it up there, yet, so she felt less awkward about walking around and talking to herself.

"Don't make a real point of cleaning you guys off, do they?" she asked one stone, perched at a kind of jaunty angle and covered in weeds. The stone had crumbled too much for her to read the name or date. She had online friends in her Abandoned Places Facebook group who loved to go trekking in the mountains and countryside and find old, forgotten cemeteries. They'd do rubbings on the stones. Taryn loved the way they looked.

"How come I never do anything like that anymore?" she asked herself aloud. "How come I don't get out and explore, or have fun like I used to?"

Suddenly, she was inexplicably angry with herself. Since the whole ghost thing started with Miss Dixie a year ago she hadn't felt like herself. And now, with these EDS symptoms getting more and more prevalent (seemed like something new every day) it felt like she was living in someone else's body. She barely recognized herself anymore. It had been so long since she'd spent the day as she wanted without thought to pain, nausea, vomiting, dizziness, whether she was too hot or too cold, blood pressure spikes (or dips), and fainting. On her bad days it was hard to get out of bed. And she was someone who used to go hiking, had camped out near the Grand Canyon with Matt in college and hiked five miles in the blazing heat of the desert!

On her good days she worked nonstop, from the minute she woke up until she went to bed, trying to squeeze in as much as possible just in case she didn't get another chance for awhile. The only reason she was doing so well at Shaker Town now was because her orthopedist had given her injections in her back and hip before she left and she'd found a decent combination of nerve pain meds and ant-inflammatories to take. But who the hell wanted to be on pain meds for the rest of their lives?

Sighing in frustration, Taryn continued on among the headstones, trying to read names when she could and bending over to pull up weeds when they were as tall as her. To a taller monument, nearly her size, she peered down and studied the inscription. "Hello, Morgan," she introduced herself. "What did you do to deserve a few extra inches?" Then she giggled at her own small joke, a foreign sound to her since she wasn't normally the giggling type.

The crabgrass scratched at her feet and she was sneezing from the goldenrods when she stumbled over something thin and papery. When she looked down Taryn jumped a mile and screeched a little, the sound echoing off the hill. Sure, the snake was already *out* of the skin but the sucker had to be at least three feet long. "Okay, that's enough of that," she muttered.

Taryn didn't do snakes.

She walked back through the field, gingerly watching her step and studying the ground beneath her, just waiting for a pissed off rattler or Copperhead to come slithering after her, armed with revenge. He had to have a brother somewhere. As her grandmother always said, when it comes to snakes where there's one, there's two.

Ironically, she could handle a few ghosts but the idea of things that could strike or sting her just scared the hell out of her. Eh, she never claimed to be logical.

After being at the park for a few days Taryn realized that if she

didn't do a supply run soon she'd go out of her mind. She would need to make a town run, for everyone else's sake if not her own. Nobody deserved to be around her without chocolate or caffeine in her system. The small refrigerator she'd lugged to her room (very un-Shakeresque but a girl had cravings) was empty. She couldn't afford to keep buying drinks from the vending machine. While she was out she'd try to throw in some fruit, too, just to make it look good. Taryn had no idea why she thought she needed to impress the store clerks but she did.

On her way down the stairs she couldn't help but remember Julie's words about the man.

Before anyone popped in, Taryn squatted down and lifted the rug away. Sure enough, a two by four feet patch of wooden boards that was definitely a different shade from the ones around it greeted her. These were new, fresh looking. The other boards were much more careworn, darker and scratched with age.

Shrugging, Taryn covered the spot back up with the rug. Well, maybe during the renovation something had happened. And then, maybe not. Maybe someone really had been murdered there and his blood had stained the floor so badly it couldn't be cleaned. Mother Ann would've approved of this. She once told a fellow Believer to "Clean your room well; for good spirits will not live where there is dirt."

But what about bad spirits? Taryn was concerned. Floors and walls didn't forget things, even if humans did move on.

The closest store was a scenic ten-minute drive away. The countryside in that part of Kentucky was some of the prettiest she'd ever seen, with its gently rolling hills, old stone fences, and abundant farmland. It reminded her a lot of what she'd seen in western Ireland.

Although she was broke more often than not Taryn dreamed of buying a big plot of land and planting a garden, getting some animals. The fact that she had a black thumb and the only fish she'd ever owned had died within twenty-four hours of bringing him home didn't deter the dream. After Andrew died, setting up shop in downtown Nashville seemed like a great idea. She'd be close to the live music venues, could pop out to eat at a host of places at 2 in the morning, and would never feel lonely surrounded by so many people

The fact was, though, she'd never felt more lonely in her life. She didn't know a single one of her neighbors by name, was a lightweight and drunk after a drink or two so clubbing wasn't

57

as much fun as it used to be, and sometimes getting out to eat that late just gave her indigestion.

The Dollar General Store, with its bright yellow sign and crowded parking lot, was something Taryn could always count on no matter where she was working. She traveled through the aisles with the rickety buggy, tossing things in as they called to her: a 6-carton of Ale-8s, a box of crackers, half a dozen candy bars, *People* magazine, shampoo, some rubber bands for her hair...

While she waited in line behind a young woman with a baby she listened to the small-town gossip going on around her. "Are these any good?" the woman currently checking out asked the check-out girl, gesturing to a pack of juice.

"Well, you know Amy Hawkins?" the cashier, probably in her early twenties, answered. "Works at Kathy's?"

"Yeah."

"Well, her brother came in here the other night and bought one in every flavor. So he liked 'em," she shrugged.

That seemed to be good enough for the other woman so she set three more up on the counter.

When the lady with the baby moved forward the cashier immediately went into a tirade with her about the local "Welcome" sign. "Did you see that somebody vandalized the Burgin sign?" the cashier demanded, her bubblegum snapping.

"I know it," the lady replied, raising her voice over her little one's fussing. "Bunch of hoodlums, if you ask me. Probably the same ones breaking into places and stealing the copper pipes and tools and stuff. Who do you think it was?"

Taryn waited patiently while they speculated, running down a list of local ingrates.

At last, it was Taryn's turn. As she handed the cashier the small stack of magazines she'd picked, she waited while she scanned each one and then took the time to read the headlines. "Hey, what do you think about these people right here?" she asked, pointing at a picture of a famous reality TV couple.

"I think they're faking it for the cameras?" Taryn offered.

"*Me* too!" she exclaimed. Turning to the man in line behind Taryn, she polled him as well. "Do you watch any of this stuff?"

"Not really," he shrugged. "My wife watches it, though. That and the Home and Garden channel."

Taryn walked out of the store feeling like she'd had more social interaction than she'd had in weeks.

By the time she'd checked out the movies at Redbox and headed back to the village she realized she wasn't quite ready to go home. With her CD player turned up on Patty Loveless, Taryn rolled down her car windows and sang along with "Lonely Too Long" as she sped down the US-68. The cashier at the store told her the road went down to the river and over a bridge and she thought she might like to take a picture of that.

And the road definitely dipped down. And down and down. Taryn was almost sea sick by the time she reached the water. She hadn't been on that bad of a road in a very long time. Squeezing her car into a slender spot by the side of the road, she eased out and held her breath, hoping she'd make it to the grass

59

before another car went by. It was kind of a deathtrap, getting out and walking around there.

The river was pretty, though, with the palisades. A few fisherman were out on it in little motorboats, hats pulled low on their heads and rods bobbing up and down with the rhythm of the water.

The sun was starting to set when Taryn walked back to her car and started to slide back in. A glint in the trees caught her eyes, however, and she decided she'd do just a tiny bit of investigating before she left.

It didn't take long for her to discover that it was a house that had been winking at her. A rambling structure, three stories if she was counting right, it was empty and hadn't been lived in for years. In fact, she wasn't entirely sure it had ever been finished. Nature had taken over and kudzu wound around it, through it, choking the doors and windows and squeezing it with a gentle but steely grip. The whole left side was covered with the awful vine, so much so that she couldn't see what was under it; it simply looked like a big stack of boxes someone had thrown a bright green blanket over. The leaves were so thick and plentiful that Taryn thought a giant might have been able to walk on the building blocks they made.

She yearned to go inside, take some shots, and explore it. But it was April, it was warm, and there were lots of places for creepy crawlie things to hide. In the end, she decided to return if Matt came up to visit. There was safety in numbers, even if snakes couldn't count.

It was closing time and all but those tourists spending the night were gone. Dustin and Lydia were pulling out as she pulled in, leaving her disappointed that she wouldn't have anyone to visit with. It was Julie's night off.

No matter, though, she thought. She had work to do. She could pop in her movie and finish her sketching in her room. It wasn't like she didn't have things to keep her occupied. And she still needed to call Matt back.

But Taryn was lonely.

T hanks to her picture taking earlier that afternoon, Miss

Dixie's battery was depleted. Before hopping into the shower Taryn took it out and plugged the battery in above the little desk.

She turned the shower on in the small bathroom and let the hot water flow but, once undressed, decided her muscles and joints ached too much to stand; a bath would be better. She poured a cup full of Epsom salt into the hot water and soon the mirror was cloudy from the steam.

Taryn lowered herself into water hot enough to scald most people and let herself sink up to her nose in bubbles. She was the only one staying in her building that night after all, the couple had checked out, and she felt oddly alone; isolated despite the fact there were people on the other side of the park eating dinner.

It was growing dark outside and the lanterns were already on, illuminating the pathways. She wanted to get outside and take some nighttime shots but would need to wait for a full moon to get the proper lighting. Her best flash broke in March and she hadn't earned enough money yet to replace it. She hoped this job would pay all her bills and let her treat herself. Her photography was just a hobby since it didn't earn her any money but she couldn't give it up; it was the most important thing in the world to her. Well, after Matt of course.

From the bedroom she could hear her phone ring as if on cue, the love theme from *The Princess Bride*. It was Matt, calling her back once she hadn't gotten back in touch with him. It rang three times then stopped. He didn't leave a message. She thought about getting out, bringing the phone to the bath, and returning his call but she was too relaxed. She might even doze a little, wait until the water was tepid before getting out.

Taryn closed her eyes and stretched her tired legs out in front of her, moaning a little as her muscles relaxed. The Shakers would definitely not approve of such a luxury, although they surely had to bathe themselves at some point. They did have bath houses, after all.

So relaxed was she that when her bedroom door opened, the tiniest of sounds, she didn't even flinch. It was a faraway noise, not part of her world. On some level she was aware of the heavy footsteps that stomped across her floor, around her bed, but they didn't faze her; she was lost in a world of soft music that played through her head and the memory of a warm summer day that wasn't hers.

The air might have changed, gotten a little cooler. Later she would remember feeling a drop of temperature even through the hot water of her bath. Deep breathing pulsated rhythmically as the thing in her bedroom wandered. And searched. This thing, no longer alive or human, could sense her, smell her, and even taste her when it opened its mouth and flicked out its serpent tongue. Its dry, cracked lips bled, with little drops falling to the ground and vanishing as soon as they touched the wood. Its claws, no longer hands, curled up and clenched, imagining her smooth white skin torn, bruised and bleeding under them. Her aroma was everywhere and it sought it out, inhaling her hairbrush on the bureau, her lavender bra tossed over the ladder-back chair, her discarded cotton underwear on the floor...With each breath it took in it wanted more and so it snarled in anger, eyes flashing and black as coal. So close, so close...

Someone's in my room, Taryn thought dreamily, feeling the water swirl around her stomach.

Someone's in my room!?

In a flash she broke from her reverie and sat up straight, ears alert. The noise, then. It had stopped. She sensed that whatever had been there was gone now but, oh, whatever it was had left something behind—something blistering and pungent. She gagged a little, the fermented scent assaulting her nose, mouth, and skin all at once. Her room was pitch black now. She'd forgotten to leave on a light and there was no moon shining through the window. Aware of her nakedness and defenselessness, not even a curling iron to whack anyone over the head with, she held her breath and trained her ears to the sounds. The footsteps had stopped but she thought she could hear breathing, male and rugged.

Oh my God, she moaned inwardly. *At least two different people have tried to kill me and now I am going to die in the bathtub.*

Her heartbeat was so loud she could hear it in her ears, a rushing sound that made her shake her head to clear it away.

Although nothing moved beyond her, there was a rhythmic undulation in the walls, a sliver of electrical energy that made the tiny hairs on her arms stand at point. Whatever had been there might be gone but something else was there now and, what's more, he or she was *aware* of her. They were both waiting to see who would make the next move.

Well, she wasn't going to go down without a fight.

Since she'd left all her toiletries in the bedroom she didn't have anything to grab onto. However, the back of the toilet did come off and she could do some serious damage with that, despite her lack of upper body strength. The element of surprise was her best bet.

In a flash, Taryn sprung from the water and grabbed at the porcelain. In one fluid movement she ran out of the bathroom, the heavy piece held high above her head by force of sheer adrenalin.

She wasn't ready for what she saw.

Above her desk, sizable sparks flew out in a show of fire. Her camera battery was aflame. The smoke was already filling the room at an alarming rate, thick and putrid. That wasn't the reason she stopped in her tracks, however.

The shadowy figure who stood by the desk had no distinct features. She could tell it was a man by height and build only. He seemed to be doing something to her wall. At first she thought he was causing the fire and she opened her mouth to scream at him, still unsure if she was seeing things or if he was a good Samaritan who'd simply broken in to help after seeing the smoke and flames from outside. But before she even had time to register what was happening the figure seemed to walk into the wall, into the flames, and they disappeared with him, as though they'd never been there at all, with only the smoke left behind.

Maintenance tried to assure her it wasn't her fault.

"You're just lucky you weren't sleeping or taking a shower," Bert, a heavyset fellow with meaty hands and a head full of wiry, gray hair, barked. "These things can get bad real fast."

Taryn was lucky she'd remembered to throw on some clothes before dialing the front desk. She'd opened the window to let the smoke out before she remembered she was still stark naked and dripping bathwater, leaving a trail of bubbles back to the bathroom.

Although there wasn't any real damage to the room she'd have to move to the other side of the building, just to give them a chance to check everything out. It didn't take her long to throw everything into her suitcases and the men helped her lug them across the hall. "You need anything?" Bert asked, a little softer now.

"I could use some caffeine," she answered.

"I've got a Coke machine by the office. It's on me if you want," he offered.

Taryn accepted gratefully and climbed into the park's golf cart.

As they roared off into the night Taryn took another look up at the building. Her window was still open; the curtain fluttered in the breeze. And a pale, lonesome face gazed down at her and watched.

CHAPTER 5

"At least you're okay," Matt sighed into the phone.

"You're lucky, though, that you weren't out when it happened."

"I know; I've thought about that," Taryn admitted. Losing her stuff would've been awful but the historic building burning to the ground would've been worse.

She hadn't told him about the figure in her room or the sounds that alerted her to the fire in the first place. She was sick and tired of thinking about ghosts. Sometimes she just wanted to move on to something else. They'd never been a part of her life until a year ago and now it felt like they were all she thought about.

"Any chance you can come up and see me?" she asked and then felt instantly guilty. He'd taken more than a month off back in the fall. And it wasn't like she was clingy or needy. She just missed his company.

"I looked at plane tickets for the end of the month," Matt replied. "I might be able to make it then. I'll know tomorrow when we have our meeting."

Matt didn't think his department could run without him. He was probably right. She could have taken a day or two off and gone to Florida to see him but Taryn just wasn't really into the area where he lived. The suburb outside of Orlando was nice, and he had a good little house she felt comfortable in, but it was blazing hot even in the spring and she always felt like she was swimming through the air. Matt preferred his house to be dark, too, to help keep it cool so the curtains were always pulled tightly together. When Taryn was there she felt like she was living in a cold, dark cave.

On the plus side, he did enjoy cooking and she always left having gained at least three pounds.

"I meant to tell you," Matt broke in, interrupting her thoughts. "I had a dream about you last night."

"Was it a dirty one?" she teased him.

"Not that time. It actually disturbed me."

"Yikes. What was I doing?" she asked with interest. Matt's dreams were normally abstract, a collection of colors and scenes that had no real plot or direction.

"You were running, crying," he worried in a strangled voice. "I could see you and hear you but couldn't get to you. There was someone after you."

"Well that doesn't sound nice," she tried to joke, but felt unsettled. "Did you see what he looked like?"

"No, faceless I guess. What bothered me was—" he stopped talking and laughed a little strangled sound.

"What?" Taryn pressed. He couldn't stop *now*.

"Oh, it's strange. I could see you running and I could see him after you but for a second it was like I was him. And I could feel what he was feeling." Matt stopped talking again, took a drink of something, then continued. "He wanted you. He wanted to touch you, grab you, put his hands everywhere. But there was rage, too. I've never felt so angry myself but it was just consuming him. He wanted to tear you apart. And I felt that."

"Geeze, Matt," Taryn laughed nervously. "Are you hiding something from me?" Although it was kind of funny to think of cool-as-a-cucumber Matt trying to hurt her.

"Oh, God n-no," Matt stuttered, aghast. "I've never felt like that in my life, not even when people cut me off in parking lots and you *know* how mad that makes me. This was something else. It just lasted for a teeny second and then I was awake. But I felt terrible, like it was my fault he was chasing you. I don't know. I didn't like it. It's been on my mind all day."

"There's nobody after me here," Taryn assured him. "Everyone is real nice and I don't think anyone is going to be chasing me any time soon. I know how to scream, anyway, and can kick like a mule."

"Yeah, well, still..." Matt, who had pulled her out of more scrapes than either would like to admit, was not entirely

69

convinced. "Just watch yourself. Evil comes in many forms and you of all people should be aware of that."

Taryn's new room looked pretty much like her other one did, sans the big black smudge above the desk and lack of suffocating smoke smell.

She knew she should be worried about the building but she was also concerned that they'd try to dock her pay for what had happened, despite the fact the park director had assured her it wasn't her fault. "It happened a few months ago to a television set in the room across the hall from you," Virgil told her cheerfully. "Wasn't a thing in the world you did."

Still, she felt responsible. She did not want to be known as the woman who burnt down Shaker Town.

They'd offered to move her to a room in The Trustee's Office and while she liked the idea of being close to the food, it was also *too* close to everyone else. There would always be a constant flurry of activity there and she wasn't feeling into that at the moment.

The figure in her other room...it was just a ghost. Ha, she laughed aloud. A year ago to see such a thing and have the thought of "he's just a ghost" run through her mind would've had her questioning her sanity. But she'd seen a lot since then and learned even more. Not all ghosts are real; some are just residual energy. Not all ghosts are aware of what's going on around them; they were just out there minding their own dead business.

But this one knew *she* was there. He could sense her, feel her. She'd known that while she was helpless in the bathtub.

But, then again, he (or maybe it was a *she* but Taryn didn't think so) had helped her. Of course, he could have just been trying to keep his building from burning down and didn't give a flip about her...

Was it possible there were *two* ghosts? She thought maybe there was. For that brief moment she'd been aware in the tub, she'd known vicious fear, something that paralyzed her on a primal level. But the figure in her room had just surprised her, made her curious.

Shaker Town was old. Lots of people had come through it. It would be more of a surprise if it wasn't haunted than it if was.

Miss Dixie stared at her from the middle of the bed. Even in the shadows of the early morning she looked taunting and accusatory at Taryn. "Pick me up," she seemed to cry. "Turn me on and you'll get the bigger picture."

"You never give me any answers," Taryn complained aloud, but still picked the camera up, the weight somehow comforting. "You just cause a lot of problems."

But ghost hunting seemed to have become Taryn's second job, and one that was starting to become more necessary.

71

Letting out a deep breath, Taryn slung the strap over her shoulder, stuffed some snacks in her knapsack, and slipped on her sandals. She had work to do, in more ways than one.

There was always a lull at some point in the day, usually around lunch, when the tourists went off to unpack their picnics or eat in the restaurant and the park got quiet. It didn't last long but it was nice while it did.

Taryn used this time to do a little more exploring and put Miss Dixie back to the test. Although Taryn had only really picked up on the one picture, so far, now that she'd seen a few things she hoped she might get more.

She'd start with the biggest building at the park, the Centre Family Dwelling.

The building, back in the day, would've been a sight to see. Not only was it imposing, it contained fairly stunning design ideas. Probably housing nearly one hundred Shakers at once, it still had the separate doors for men and women. Interior walls had "borrowed light" which allowed in air and sunlight. It also had a dumbwaiter, separate stair cases for the sexes inside, food storage rooms, a large dining room, and a kitchen with all the latest nineteenth century technology for food preparation.

When she walked through the front entrance she could hear laughter back in the old kitchen but there wasn't anyone in the front of the building. There were some interesting rooms down there but while she still had the energy she wanted to start at the top.

The stairs were hard on Taryn's legs so she took them slowly, willing herself not to sublux her hip or, worse, dislocate it altogether. The Ehlers-Danlos Syndrome could and did do that frequently and today it was making her joints hurt worse than usual so she was trying to be easy on herself, especially her hips and legs which seemed to hurt the worst. She had just turned thirty-one a month before but felt twice that.

The top floor was deathly quiet, not a soul to be seen or heard.

Before that could change she quickly turned Miss Dixie on and began walking through the rooms, paying careful attention to zoom in on the beds, the chairs, and anywhere a person might turn their attention to. As someone known for being messy Taryn was hypnotized by the Shakers' fastidiousness. Mother Ann had even lectured the Believers to "be neat and industrious; keep your family's clothes clean and decent; see that your house is kept clean, and your victuals is prepared in good order" and to not lose anything, waste anything, or carry debt. With their pegs for everything and cleanliness-is-next-to-Godliness mentality they were truly Matt's kind of people.

Taryn fantasized about selling or donating everything she had and living Spartan-style in a tiny house she could take on the road with her but knew that wasn't realistic. What would she do without her record or cowboy boot collections?

Even though the Shakers hadn't had an official church, per say, the cavernous rooms with their hushed quietness and tidiness reminded her of a chapel. The click of her camera was so loud that it echoed, making her jump once. She slowly moved from one room to another, aiming and shooting until she'd covered the top floor. One piece of furniture struck her as both sweet and a little funny; a large cradle rested in the middle of the floor, a blanket and pillow inside. Although she could have easily fit inside it, it wasn't made for a large baby...they'd used these adult cradles for the older Shakers who were sick or disabled and needed comforting.

When the bell rang to signify the commencement of the singing, Taryn smiled. Lydia was off so it was a male voice that filled the course between the two buildings when she started on the floor beneath her. His voice was a rich, even baritone and though she'd learned most of the songs on the program since her arrival she still appreciated the stunning beauty of the voice and lyrics. If there was anyone left in the building, now, they'd make their way out and find themselves in the meeting house. It was hard to ignore the singing.

She stopped in what was set up like a children's room and gave herself a moment, just taking in the tiny wooden toys and small beds and chairs. Did children's cries echo in here, after being taken away from their mothers and fathers? She tried to imagine a child who'd lived in the same room as their parents suddenly tugged away and cast alone in a strange room with other children they didn't know. Had it been frightening or exciting, a new adventure for them? As religious as they'd been the whole "go forth and multiply" hadn't pertained to the Shakers. It was only through bringing in converts or taking in orphans that they'd been able to sustain their population.

Even though Taryn hadn't been close to her parents, she'd still mourned them when they'd died; she'd felt like an orphan. They were *good* people, just distant. She'd preferred living with her grandmother but couldn't imagine the idea of being torn apart from them while they were living. What had it been like for the children here, to see their parents on the other side and not be able to go to them, hug them, stay with them?

Taryn imagined that those rules were frequently broken, probably by the mothers.

A scraping noise behind her made her jump a little. It was the sound of furniture moving across the wooden floors. Since children were encouraged to touch things and even play in that room Taryn turned and expected to find a little one at her feet. The expectant smile on her face disappeared, however, when she was met with nothing but a cold draft of air that shot across her face and lifted the hair off her shoulders.

Something passed through her, something malicious and unforgiving that clutched at her insides and scratched until she thought she would scream and it finally gave up and slithered out on the other side.

Though not someone she would consider to be maternal, her instinct was to turn and protect the long-ago children who had once (maybe) filled the small room behind her. The thickness that permeated the space around her was pure, unadulterated evil and Taryn recognized it for what it was. The pictures on the wall shook a little, a small chair fell over as the presence traveled around the room, searching for something it couldn't find. She saw the quilt on the bed slide to the floor in an untidy heap and it filled her with anger that something so ugly would even dare to touch the innocence of childhood.

"Get out of here," she hissed but even as she spoke her fingers slid across her camera, snapping a picture so that the flash of light filled the room at once and set even the dark corners ablaze with light.

The putrid air passed through her again, this time in a frantic rush so that she stumbled backwards into the doorjamb and nearly toppled to the floor.

The air was still once again, unbroken by scent or sound or noise. She waited, though, and gathered herself. There were footsteps on the stairs now and someone would be up in a moment.

Giving one last look at the small room, Taryn had the urge to pull the door to, to keep out anything that might be lurking outside. She left it open to the light, however, and hoped whatever had been there had passed.

She was barely in the foyer when the smothered sound of giggles erupted from the empty room behind her.

Her hands caked with acrylic paint and her hair plastered to

her head with sweat, Taryn was anxious to return to her room for a shower before heading to the other building to catch supper. The temperature had dropped a little but the humidity was still high, causing her clothes to stick to her body. Although she was tired, achy, and more than a little messy Taryn couldn't complain. In the twilight of the day the sun was casting a colorful quilt over the low-rising hills and valleys and everything moved just a little bit more slowly, deliberately.

Her grandmother had called this the "magic hour," and when she was little Taryn thought that meant fairies and unicorns came out to play. She would sit on the porch of her suburban Nashville street, peering over the rooftops of the houses that surrounded her, hoping to catch a glimpse of something magical. Even as a teenager she'd sometimes sit on the back porch of her grandmother's home in nearby Franklin, surrounded by her potted tomato plants and butterfly bushes in the summertime and pretend the fairies really might come out to play.

Now, Taryn just enjoyed the walk back to her building, her knapsack hanging low on her back and her art supplies slung over her shoulder in a black leather satchel.

Still, the chill of her experience in the children's room hadn't left her. She'd worn it all day and on occasion the decay of whatever the essence had been wafted up from her clothing, assaulting her all over again. She'd found herself paranoid a few times, sure someone was standing just inches behind her while she painted or was watching her from behind a row of trees. There was never anyone there, though, and the tourists who were interested in her work kept a respectable (but visible) distance.

Her room was cold when she entered and Taryn welcomed the air, although it immediately chilled the dampness on her skin. Shrugging off her capris and T-shirt she slipped on her bathrobe and sat down on the bed to go through her pictures.

Most were unremarkable but when she got to the second floor of the Centre Family Dwelling she paused and zoomed in, looking carefully. In real life, the beds in the first bedroom were on the east side of the room and there were four of them. Miss Dixie, however, showed three on the west. They were still neatly made up, with white coverlets and orderly pillows. A chair hung on a wall peg and two pairs of sturdy shoes lined the floor under a window.

These had not been there earlier.

Still taken aback every time her camera showed her a change, Taryn shook her head, trying to clear the clutter in her mind. It made zero sense to her that she would see some things yet not others. The next three photographs were normal, without any deviation from what she'd seen outside of the lens.

And then there was the children's room. It was still the children's room through her camera, with the same small bed and chairs and costumes laid out for guests to try on. That wasn't any different. In the center of the room, however, was a tall, shadowy figure of a man. His arms were stretched out powerfully, as though opening himself to whatever might befall him. Although Taryn could see *through* him, there was still something fierce about his stance, the ethereal lines of his body did not lessen the power of his manifestation. Indeed, the objects in the room around him were wavy, a little unclear, as though his presence weakened them.

But, maybe worst of all, his savage glare was directed straight at Taryn.

CHAPTER 6

*T*aryn spent the next four nights tossing and turning

in her sleep, unable to achieve any quality rest. Her days were a blur of unseasonable heat, linseed oil, and frantic strokes of color on canvas. One of the buildings was almost complete. She was saving the school building for last, since it was in the worst shape, and she'd need to do more research on it to reconstruct it.

On her iPod Taryn played the high-energy songs of Bruce Springsteen, Bon Jovi, and John Mellencamp. She considered these her "blue collar threesome." She was normally more of an alt-country fan but when her energy was low she needed something that would get her blood pumping. It just made her work faster.

People were friendly enough, and even stopped to talk and invite her to lunch, but when the work was moving swiftly she preferred to be alone and stay inside her own head. Ellen, the server who waited on her the most, took to bringing Taryn her lunch outside when she didn't show up in time to eat, and brought her dinner once. These short interactions were about all Taryn could handle while she worked.

In the evenings she zoned out in front of the television in her room, sometimes not even aware of what was playing before her. From her bed, if she kept the curtains open, she had a beautiful view of the stars at night and she'd watch them until she dozed, thinking of how those same twinkling lights once shone on the people who lived there more than a hundred years ago.

She continued to talk to Matt throughout the day, sometimes by phone and sometimes by messenger. His work was moving along and he was in the middle of some project. He always sounded distracted, even when he was at home, so she tried not to bother him much.

She ate her meals at a small table in the restaurant by herself, tasting very little of the wonderfully southern fare yet filling up just the same.

And something continued to stalk her.

"This is Andy Tribble," Dustin announced, introducing Taryn

to the middle-aged man who stood beside him. Next to beanpole Dustin, Andy was short and stubby, his belly protruding over his pants so far that Taryn couldn't see his belt properly. He looked to be around fifty and Taryn was almost certain that the lopsided thick patch of hair on his head was not truly his.

"Hello," he wheezed, holding out his soft, beefy hand that swallowed hers. His was wet from sweat and instantly dampened her palm. She resisted the urge to wipe it on her skirt. But, after all, she didn't want to be rude. Grinning, he pushed his large glasses back up on his nose, leaving a cloudy patch of moisture from his finger on the glass. "Hot, ain't it?"

"Just a bit," she smiled politely although, indeed, it was a scorcher. Taryn was wearing a short, pink peasant skirt and white tank top. Although both were cotton and lightweight the sweat beads were still rolling down her back and stomach, gathering on her legs.

"Andy is here to write a book about the Shakers of Pleasant Hill," Dustin explained.

Andy bobbed his head in excitement. "About their methods of acquiring new members," he proclaimed. "It's for the University Press."

"Will you be living here while you write the book?" Taryn asked politely.

They were standing in the middle of the gravel road that ran through the park and although they were shaded by the big, leafy trees her legs were killing her and she couldn't wait to sit down and have a drink. She'd been on her way to the restaurant for lunch when Dustin stopped her.

"Oh, no, no," he shook his head, his hair flapping with the movement. "I live in Harrodsburg. But I'll be out here every day," he promised.

"Andy has some interesting ideas about the Shakers," Dustin admitted, a hint of a smile on his lips. "Especially about the ghosts."

"Oh, well, I guess I do," Andy admitted. "I'm more of a realist and intellectual about these things. I don't, for instance, think the Shakers really had religious experiences during their meetings."

"Well," Taryn pointed out, "they didn't have religious experiences at every meeting. Some days of the week the meetings were just for going over their finances. And then there were meetings where letters from other societies were read. Some nights it would have been a union meeting *just* for conversation. And one day of the week they had to get together to learn any new songs and dances. They really only used one day of the week for all the stomping around, marching, and singing we know them for. Sometimes they just talked." Taryn was lecturing now, in full tour guide mode.

Andy's face reddened even more, turning a deep shade of purple. Ignoring everything she'd just said he sputtered, "And I think there's *always* a reasonable explanation for ghosts."

Now feeling a little prickly, maybe from the heat and maybe from his bull, Taryn cocked her head and studied the little man in front of her. "I think there's a reasonable explanation for ghosts, too," she pronounced with authority.

"Yeah, what's that?"

"That somebody died and now they're haunting a place."

Andy's face reddened, Dustin snickered, and Taryn politely smiled, resisting the urge to flutter her eyelashes.

Later, back in the archive room, Taryn felt guilty for being

rude to the poor man and told herself she'd apologize and make it up to him the next time she saw him. After all, he was as entitled to his opinions as she was to hers. She remembered what the owner of Windwood Farm had told her the first time she met him–that maybe she didn't believe in ghosts because she'd never seen one.

Obviously, that had changed.

Taryn smiled to herself now, remember the naiveté she'd walked into *that* job with. And at how quickly things had changed for her.

The sun was setting when she started putting books back and organizing her belongings. The small green lamp on the desk flickered once, then went out, leaving her in a stuffy darkness, the smell of books musty combined with the dust and wooden shelves.

Taryn stopped what she was doing and rooted around for her cell phone. It was at the bottom of her bag and by the time she found it the room had magically grown almost completely dark; not even the outline of the furniture was visible.

Snapping her phone open, the small blue light illuminated the close quarters and offered some comfort. Taryn was a little claustrophobic and a whole lot afraid of the dark so she welcomed its glow. She quickly stuffed the rest of her papers into her knapsack and threw it over her shoulder and, still holding onto her phone, was halfway to the door when a sound caught her in her tracks.

Taryn hesitated mid step, not sure if she wanted to turn around and look or not. It was just a slight shuffling noise, and on the other side of the room, but it was the unmistakable sound of a fabric rustling against something. A breath caught then, Taryn was never sure whose it was, and the room filled with the slow, sweet voice of song.

This wasn't the vibrato of the docents in the meeting house, with their powerful voices and theatrics. This was a sweet, soft voice that first sang with hesitation and then grew with confidence as the words swirled around Taryn like tiny daggers pricking at her skin.

"Twas in the merry month of May/When all gay flowers were blooming..." the voice rang out, oblivious to their audience.

The sad words and melancholy melody fell flatly against the darkness, swallowed up by time and space. Taryn couldn't help herself; she *had* to listen. The other woman might have been dead but her voice was young, almost hopeful, and innocent. It was impossible to turn away from.

Unlike the blast of air that had accosted her days before, this time Taryn was consumed with a yearning that was much stronger than any fear that might have settled over her. The rustling continued as well and it was then Taryn realized the figure must have been pacing back and forth, carrying on a task that had seen its completion a long time ago.

Biting her lip and holding her breath, Taryn turned then and searched for the spirit with her eyes. The glow of the cell phone faltered for a moment, and then, in the murky shadows, it lit on a pale, blue dress and the even paler silhouette of a woman even younger than herself. She wasn't quite solid, as the light appeared to shine through her, but she was as real as anything Taryn had ever seen.

She appeared not to notice Taryn at all as she continued the pacing and singing, wringing something in her long, elegant fingers.

Taryn began the process of untangling Miss Dixie from around her neck when she was struck once again by the cold, savage wind. It didn't move through her this time, but *around* her, and Taryn could see the moment when it struck the other woman. With a muffled shout, the woman fell backwards, clawing at the air, and Taryn watched in horror as her face distorted first into fear and then pain. She screamed, struggled, and pleaded for help but her invisible attacker showed her no mercy. Taryn reached for her but an invisible wall separated them; Taryn couldn't get through. Then, the woman's eyes rolled back and her head fell limply to one side. *She's dead for sure now*, Taryn thought helplessly, nervous laughter and fear making her retch. The last thing Taryn saw before darting out the door, into the light, was the shadowy figure falling upon the apparition, stamping her out like an eclipse.

There were more than a dozen messages from Matt back in her room. Some of them were chatty diatribes about his day, how much he missed her, and his puttering around the house. He was trying for an herb garden in his kitchen this year and wanted her advice on heirloom tomatoes for his backyard garden. And then there were his funny cat videos, singing hamsters, and comedic sketches. Matt was a pro at procrastinating and liked to send everything he came across her way.

Taryn sat there and stared at her computer screen, trying to figure out what to write in response.

"Dear Matt, Saw a woman get attacked today. It's all cool, though, because she was already dead."

That seemed a little harsh.
Or,

"Dear Matt, Felt some scary wind today and it smelled real bad, too."

No, that just made it sound like she had bad gas.
How about:

"Dear Matt, Met a guy who just completely rubbed me the wrong way so I snapped at him."

That made her look hateful.

In the end she just sent him back a short note, talked about her painting and research, and left it at that. She knew he'd read it and sense something else, Matt was good at reading what she didn't say as much as what she did, but she'd cross that bridge when she got there. She was still shaking from the murder she'd witnessed, the panic and fear on the other woman's face. The helplessness of the situation. *Why hadn't someone helped her*, Taryn cried to herself. Where was everyone?

She'd been dreading the walk back to her building but it was Friday night and the weather was nice. The guestrooms were almost completely full so others had been walking back to their accommodations as well. She'd blended in with a couple of tourists and stayed with them until she'd reached her floor. Even doing that, though, she'd felt an impending sense of dread with almost every step she took.

Now, back in her room, her fluffy housecoat was wrapped snugly around her, protecting her, and a comedy droned on the television. Taryn played around on the internet, trying different terms to plug into Google. Looking for deaths at Shaker Town, murders at Shaker Town, or even Shaker ghosts wasn't getting her anywhere. Of course there were deaths here; people moved in and many stayed until they died. And, according to the search engine at least, murders apparently just didn't happen. She knew better, but figured that even back then there were probably cover ups. News of a murder would have definitely affected enrollment of the newbies. Several sites, and even a couple of books, had write ups about Shaker ghosts but they were either in a general sense or had nothing to do with the lady she'd seen.

She was at a standstill.

On the one hand, Taryn could totally get on board with many of the Shaker ideals. After all, it was in many ways a feminist-based religion, built more on spirituality than doctrine. The Shakers had believed in gender equality, fairness, and having a personal relationship with God. The founder, Ann Lee, though considered a little loopy by some had been filled with some fascinating visions and occultist fanaticism, many of which she used to help form the ideals of her followers. Taryn, also being someone who could see the dead, had to respect a woman who not only communicated with spirits but built an entire religion around it.

Unlike the Amish, another group she was fascinated with, they not only embraced modern technology (at Pleasant Hill the women had a horse-charged washing machine) but were the first to use many advancements in the area.

There had to have been a dark side, however. Religious groups of any kind always drew extremists. And, as much as she respected the Shakers and adored the grounds and park, in today's world you had to admit they would've been seen as a cult. Albeit, a friendly and sociable one. During her research she came across stories of families joining together and one parent wishing to leave the order while the other one stayed. Vicious custody fights ensued, with the children trapped in the middle. Taryn shuddered just thinking about it.

By the time she'd fooled around online and distracted herself by falling down a few rabbit holes, it was past midnight. The movie on television had turned into some late-late-late show and a political author droned about FEMA camps, his voice monotonous and even pitched.

Taryn turned off and unplugged her laptop, it was starting to get uncomfortably hot and she was paranoid about another fire, and slipped on her nightgown. She'd just turned off the television and hopped in bed when her curtains fluttered in the window, their heaviness nearly knocking over her desk chair.

She could see from her bed that her window was closed and the air vent was on the other side of the room. Clutching her blanket up to her chin, Taryn's nerves went into overdrive as she waited with bated breath. Did she get up and check? Call someone? And say what-hey, my curtains just moved?

She waited, certain something evil and torrid was going to fill the room and briefly turn her world upside down again, but nothing happened. The curtains settled back down, falling back against the wall with a soft thud and Taryn was left alone in a quiet room.

Well, perhaps it had just been a fluke, just a gust of wind from the air conditioner picking up more speed than usual. It was chillier than it had been earlier, she suddenly realized. Her forearms were lined with goose bumps.

And then the singing began again.

Taryn knew immediately that it was the same woman she'd heard earlier, singing the same song. The voice wasn't in the room with her, but close enough that Taryn could hear her clearly.

Shaken with equal amounts of curiosity and fear, Taryn softly dropped to the floor and crossed over to her window, her beside lamp casting a comforting glow across the hardwood floor. There, on the expanse of lawn below her, the woman walked slowly in the moonlight, the ribbons of her bonnet flowing out behind her. Tendrils of blond hair, maybe brought loose by the breeze, fell against her shoulders and bobbed with her movement. This time Taryn could see that her dress was not white, but blue; it was the ethereal glowing around her that made it appear paler.

Like she had been in the archives room, she was peaceful as she moved along, humming the little tune under her breath. Taryn could catch a word and phrase now and then, a song about lost love and friends denying her because of the feelings that consumed her. It was nearly as haunting as the vision, those words and melody, and Taryn felt them go straight to her own heart. She watched as the figure picked up her pace, glancing over her shoulder quickly, and then headed towards the ruins of the old school house. And then Taryn watched as she slipped right through the walls and disappeared.

CHAPTER 7

*T*aryn had made several friends at Shaker Town, and

liked most everyone she met, but it was Julie's comments about the ghosts that had her seeking the young woman out. She had to wait until the evening, since Julie tended to work Happy Hour onward, and the day dragged by in the Kentucky heat. Taryn took far more breaks than usual, using her time unwisely, but entreatingly enough, as she strolled to the barn and babied the horses, watched the cows, and fed the ducks. Much to the confusion of a tour group, she even entertained herself for a few minutes by jogging back and forth in front of several cows, just to giggle when they turned their heads to watch her.

She created her own amusement when she was unable to find any anywhere else.

It was a little unnerving to go back and look at the schoolhouse, considering what she'd seen the night before, but now she studied it with interest. Had the woman been a teacher? Died in the building? Been attacked there? Or, had the building also been used as something else and she was going there for that purpose?

Taryn was still intimidated by the haunting aspect of the things she witnessed but the mystery part of it fascinated her. She'd trained her camera on the building several times already and hadn't picked up on a single thing but now she tried it again, carefully walking around the ruins and keeping an eye out for spiders and snakes as she did so.

When she stopped and looked back over her shot on the LCD screen she was startled to see a perfectly restored building with curtains at the window and smoke drifting from the chimney—not a brick out of place. It was a far cry from the jumble of stones and weeds it was now.

Taryn was certain, however, that the building was important in some way and was being shown to her for a reason.

Ordinarily Taryn would go inside, either by the front door or climbing through a window, and check things out. Probably aim her camera at a few corners and try to pick up on something. That wasn't a possibility here, though, since there were no windows or doors to speak of and the roof had caved in a long time ago.

Her sleuthing would have to take place somewhere else.

It was just about time for Julie to come on, though, and after waiting to see her all day Taryn paced impatiently by the building close to the parking lot, hoping to catch her before she went inside. The bee hive was above her, still alive, and the sounds were making her nervous. Why hadn't someone taken that down and relocated it already?

"Hey Julie," Taryn called, resisting the urge to run to her when she walked up the sidewalk. Taryn felt a little bit like a teenage girl stalking her crush by his locker. "I'm trying to catch you before you go. You got a minute?"

"Sure," Julie smiled, removing an ear bud and hitting a button on her phone. Julie was dressed in tight-fitting pants, a button-up sweater, and leather boots. She had an infinity scarf hanging loosely around her neck and large, dangly turquoise earrings. Her makeup was expertly applied, bringing out her large brown eyes, and her hair skimming the tops of her shoulders in a casual bob. Taryn only wished she'd ever looked half as put together. "I have a few minutes."

Now that she was in front of her, however, Taryn wasn't sure what to say without sounding like a moron. She figured the roundabout way was the best approach.

95

"Well, I've been doing some research on the schoolhouse and came across some information. I'm just trying to find out more on it," she began.

"Well, Dustin and Lydia probably know more about that. And maybe Bob James, the carpenter. He's been here forever," Julie explained.

"Yeah, well, this is kind of...sensitive," Taryn finished lamely. "I guess I was just wondering if..."

"Yeah?"

"Do you know if anyone died in that school? Or if something happened to one of the teachers?" Taryn blurted out at last.

Julie sucked in her lips in contemplation and then shrugged. "Not that I've heard of," she relented at last. "Are we talking ghosts here?"

"Yeah, we are," Taryn admitted. "I keep seeing this woman, and hearing her sing. Last night she went inside the school. I just thought that maybe she was a teacher. Or got killed in there."

"I know a few of the ghost stories around here, but nothing involving a woman. People have seen her, like I said, but nobody's ever come up with any explanation as to who she is."

Taryn considered this. Perhaps she'd have to take a different approach. "What about murders? Anything like that? I tried to do some research online but couldn't come up with anything."

"Well," Julie lowered her voice even though there wasn't anyone else around. "They don't like to talk about this but one of the elders was killed sometime around 1840," she whispered.

"By who? And how?" Taryn was whispering too and felt a little guilty, like they were gossiping, despite the fact the alleged victim died more than one hundred fifty years before.

"I don't know how. Strangled, hit over the head with something?" Julie replied vaguely. "And nobody seems to know who did it, although I think the general consensus was that it was one of the 'world's people.'"

"Not a Shaker then?"

Julie laughed. "And if it was then that would've been hushed up real fast."

Taryn laughed along with her and watched as Julie sobered. "Look, there's another ghost story here, one you probably don't want to know. It's, well, totally morbid."

"Yeah?"

"Some people over in Harrodsburg and Burgin say that there's a pond nearby and that the Shakers would kill kids, mostly babies, and throw their bodies in the pond," Julie chirped and then blushed, like she'd just been caught smoking in church.

"What?" Taryn yelped, startled. "The Shakers wouldn't have killed anyone."

"Yeah, I know," Julie said, but didn't look convinced. "But people say they can hear the babies crying at night. And that, supposedly, the pond was drained and skeletons were found. A lot of them."

"It wouldn't have made sense for the Shakers to kill kids," Taryn mused, mostly to herself. "Their population grew by encouraging folks to join. I mean, the little windows in the meeting house were for the elders to sit and observe the tourists so they could find ones that might be approachable and willing to try them out. They couldn't afford to reduce their population."

"It doesn't make sense to me, either," Julie admitted. "But that's just what I've heard."

"Have you ever heard the babies crying?" Taryn asked with a shudder.

"N-no. I mean, I don't think I did. I heard something once. But it was probably a cat crying," Julie added in a rush.

George walked up then, with a look of consternation. "Doesn't anyone work around here?" he grumbled.

"Oh George, you're so grouchy," Julie teased him.

He was having none of that, though. "All you girls ever do is stand around and gossip. You don't do shit. You," he pointed at Julie, "you just flirt with men you think will give you money."

Julie's mouth dropped open and when she tried to speak, nothing would come out.

Taryn took a step closer and put her hand on his shoulder. He felt cold and stiff. "George?" she asked softly. "Are you sick?"

He turned to her then, eyes dead and vacant. "And you! You don't do anything they couldn't hire a kid with finger paints to do and they're actually paying you! What a fucking crock!"

Taryn's face paled and she took a step back. When George reached out to grab her by the wrist and yank her closer, however, there was a loud roar that filled the air and shook them all. None of them would be able to tell anyone what happened next or how it happened but the tour group who was standing nearby, waiting to go in for supper, said it looked as though the hive had just come loose and flown through the air. George was in the unfortunate location of being in the exact spot where it landed.

Because of what happened down in Georgia she was trying to learn to take care of herself more, to not depend so much on Matt. She felt like she was crossing boundaries with the ghosts even more than sleeping with him. It had nearly gotten him killed and she'd rather die herself.

But now she called him. There were times when you just needed reinforcements.

"I need help," Taryn sighed into the phone.

"You need me to come up there?" he asked with interest.

"No," Taryn retorted, a little offended. "I think we can handle it over the phone."

"Oh, sorry." Now he sounded sad. "I'm just looking for an excuse to jump ship and come see you. I miss you."

"Oh, well," Taryn softened. "I thought you couldn't leave work?"

"Turns out I am starting not to care so much. That reminds me...how would you feel about me looking for a job around Nashville? Finding a place with you. Not that your apartment isn't...lovely," he added in distaste.

"And leave NASA?" Taryn was shocked. He'd actually gone to university and studied aeronautical engineering so that he could specifically work at NASA. "I don't think you're going to find anything comparable in Nashville."

"There's a science museum or something, isn't there?" he mused. She could almost see him staring off into space, lost in his head, like he did as a child.

"Not quite the same, dude."

They were off topic now, as frequently happened, and it was up to Taryn to rein him back in. Still, it was a topic they'd eventually have to revisit. "My problem?" she asked gently.

"Right. Sorry. So what's up?"

"Shaker Town is haunted," she began grandly.

"Yeah?"

"We're not talking your typical dead people here, Matt," she sniffed. "There's the classic woman in white, the evil lurker, and maybe even dead babies this time."

"Ooooh. Well those don't sound good. Except for maybe the woman in white. She seemed okay in that Halloween movie with the creepy little kid."

"You're thinking 'The Lady in White'," Taryn reminded him. "Now I don't know about the infants. I have a feeling that might just be an urban legend. I hope to goodness it is. I can't even watch a movie where a child dies. And what we learned at Griffith Tavern about killed me."

"Well, fingers crossed on that one. I don't do dead children either. I can barely handle dead adults. So what's the issue, exactly?"

"Oh, you know, same old thing," Taryn answered. "I see dead people, my camera sees dead people, and Shaggy, there's a mystery to solve."

"What makes this one different than the others?" Matt asked with reason.

"That I don't know who or what it is I guess. And that irritates me," Taryn admitted. "The Shakers lived here for a long time and millions of people have been on the grounds. It could be anyone."

"Is there a chance the haunting is benign and has nothing to do with you? That the ghosts are just going on with their deadly business and you're just sensitive to them?" Matt asked gently.

"Maybe..."

"That maybe you're not supposed to do anything about it? We did talk about that once. That you're going to have to get used to sometimes not doing anything at all," he pointed out.

He was right, of course. Just because Miss Dixie picked up on a chair or table and just because she heard an undead concert in the middle of the night didn't mean she was being summoned for something.

"So what do I do?" she asked. "What's the sign, so to speak, that I am supposed to be waiting for? A ghost to pass me a note at dinner? Where do I draw that line?"

"I don't know, dear," Matt sighed. He sounded tired now. "I don't know. I wish I could give you all the answers."

CHAPTER 8

*T*he ride to Lexington, the biggest city closest to her,

was an eye opener. They'd told her at Guest Services that the road was "a little windy" but she thought HWY 68 might just kill her. If she wasn't afraid of slipping down over the embankment and tumbling to the river far below she was watching for other cars and praying she didn't pass any; the road was barely wide enough to be considered real.

Not that it wasn't pretty, of course. It was beautiful with its leafy green canopy, death-defying twists and turns, and towering hills. But she was awfully glad when she finally pulled into the parking lot of the Fayette Mall and got out of her car.

"Land! Land," she panted, not caring that the couple walking past her turned and gave her a strange look.

"Probably meth," the middle-aged woman whispered to the man and they picked up their pace.

There was an easier way to reach Lexington and she'd take it going back. Screw the "scenic view." Not even Patti Griffen's soothing gospel album playing on her CD player had calmed her nerves.

She'd visited Lexington while she worked at Windwood Farm and had appreciated it for its charming restaurants, beautifully restored downtown, large bookstore, and art supply stores. Although she was technically there to pick up more paint, she really just wanted to lose herself in the mall for awhile. There was nothing like a good bout of retail therapy to let yourself zone out for awhile.

Despite the mass of people, loud Muzak, and brightly-colored lights (malls rarely had dork corners) Taryn didn't think many places in the world were as lonely or artificial as indoor shopping malls. The customers always seemed to walk at either a snail's pace, kind of sauntering, or at rapid speed, ready to bulldoze anyone in their way. No matter what their pace was, they most all stared straight in front of themselves, refusing eye contact with strangers, and barely registered the fact that there were others around them. The cavernous rooms and high ceilings, coupled with the canned music, drowned out the voices so that the spaces always felt empty.

These weren't necessarily bad things to Taryn's mind. Sometimes she wanted to be amidst people but didn't necessarily want to interact. Flea markets were outdoor, social events. And sometimes she wanted that, too.

After leaving Georgia she'd returned to Florida and spent Christmas with Matt. In January, however, she'd returned back to Nashville. In addition to the fact that her savings were dwindling and she needed money, nothing at Matt's house was really hers. She was living out of her suitcases, without a dresser drawer or closet space, felt like she needed to ask permission whenever she ate something from the refrigerator or cupboard, and had nothing personal even setting around the house to help her claim it. For someone used to spending a lot of time in hotel rooms, this might have been a bit ironic but at least in the hotel rooms she could spread out, be responsible for her own mess, and create little spaces for herself.

She'd made the mistake of driving back down with Matt, too, and without a vehicle had felt isolated and cut off from the rest of the world, despite the fact he lived on a crowded street with neighbors within spitting distance on both sides.

There'd been nothing to do while she was there, other than read, watch movies, sleep, and surf the internet. And there was only so much of all three a girl could handle. She'd gotten into so many fights with what she could only imagine were teenage girls online that at least two reality TV forums had banned her. Her forty-three Facebook friends hadn't kept her very entertained. She'd taken so many pictures of the houses in Matt's neighborhood that the one evening she saw an armadillo, something different, she'd been ecstatic.

She didn't think Matt minded so much when she left, either. He hadn't put up too much of a fuss when she'd announced she needed to get back to her apartment and air it out. Before she walked out of the house she'd left her fuzzy blanket folded up on the back of his couch, a piece of her, a sign that she'd be returning soon.

Two days later it arrived in the mail with a short note that read: Oops! You forgot this!

So much for sentimentality.

A few short jobs later and her bank account was full again and for the first time in a long while she had a little bit of spending money in her pocket. Taryn strolled through the stores, munching on a hot pretzel, and tried on skirts, shorts, and soft cotton tops. She hit Bath & Body Works on a sale day and left with a bag full of bubble bath and shower gel. She got new comfortable sandals and three trashy magazines.

It was a good day; good to get out, see something new, and treat herself.

After Taryn left the mall she headed a few miles away to New

Age Gifts & More. She'd met the store owner, Rob, almost a year ago. In his store he refurbished electronics and sold an eclectic array of crystals and pentagram jewelry. He was part hippie, part Donald Trump. (Taryn later discovered he lived in one of the renovated mini-mansions behind Rupp Arena on Madison Street.) But, to her, he was now a friend and someone who'd come to her aid more than once.

"Rob!" Taryn called as she walked through the innocuous glass doors in the middle of the nondescript strip mall. Outside was a littered parking lot with rows of SUVs and sweltering pavement. Inside was an explosion of color with row after row of herbs, dream catchers, Tarot decks, and bronzed Buddha statues clashed with Xboxes, DVD players, and iPhone cases.

A shaggy head poked up from behind the counter and the young man smiled through a bushy beard. He and Matt had gone through college together, and graduated with the same degrees, but had chosen very different career paths.

"Hey! I knew it was you as soon as I heard the pretty voice," he flirted, coming out to engulf her in a great big bear hug.

Taryn knew Rob had a serious girlfriend and embraced him back out of sheer affection. He was one of the few people she felt totally comfortable with when it came to talking about her experiences. She still didn't know exactly what to do with what she had but when she talked to him it made her feel a little less awkward and freakish.

After he hung the "closed" sign on the door and they settled onto the small sofa behind the counter, Taryn felt herself relax. Rob had some kind of sweet-smelling herb on the incense burner, she was almost certain it wasn't pot, and Loreena McKennit on the CD player. Spread out around his feet were the parts to a HP printer.

"You know, it pays the bills," he shrugged, gesturing to the disarray on the floor. "So I hear you're working over there with the Shakers."

"For a little while," Taryn replied. "It was kind of a dream job. I wrote my dissertation on the Shakers, you know."

"So I'm assuming something's going on there," he prodded. Rob didn't beat around the bush.

"Well, yeah, but I wanted to see you, too. You're the only friend I have in the area," Taryn said. She left out the part where he was one of the only friends she had *period*.

"I'll take that as a compliment, although it's probably not true."

She realized then, that she did have another friend. Melissa in Vidalia, where she'd worked at Windwood Farm, was a Facebook friend now and they sometimes chatted back and forth. She hadn't even thought about trying to meet up with her while she was so close but now it sounded like a fine idea.

"So tell me what's going on over there with the cult," Rob prodded.

"It's not a cult," Taryn laughed.

"All forms of religious groups are cults in my book. No offense to them," he apologized without enthusiasm. "I know about the ghosts, though. I used to sell copies of a book about the Shaker ghosts."

Taryn perked up and straightened. "Yeah? You remember anything about them?"

"Just your usual, run-of-the-mill ghost stories. You know, creaky noises, people walking around in period clothing who weren't actually employees, singing, stuff like that."

"Any stories on who any of those people might have been?"

Rob scratched his beard, pulled out a loose hair, and studied it before tossing it into the trash. "Getting grayer every day," he grumbled. "And to answer your question, I don't think so. There may have been a story about a murder. Maybe one about a suicide. I can't really remember, though. It's been awhile. Nothing that stood out, you know?"

"What about babies?"

"You asking if I have one or you asking if I can help you have one?" he winked.

"Oh Lord, no," Taryn laughed. "Not yet. I meant babies at Shaker Town. I heard a story about a pond."

"Oh yeah!" Rob snapped his finger. "Dead babies in a pond! Oh, man, sorry about that. I get crass sometimes."

"It's okay," Taryn replied. "Is that story true? I mean, not that the Shakers killed infants but that there were skeletons in the pond?"

"I've heard that story before, that you can hear babies crying at night and people thought they were coming from the pond," Rob agreed. "But, to my knowledge, no skeletons have been found in it. That part is an urban legend."

"Thank God," Taryn murmured. "Some things are just too much."

"So tell Daddy what you're seeing," Rob encouraged her. "What's eating at you?"

"Curiosity mostly," Taryn admitted. "Not knowing what happened. Wondering who those people are, why they died, what happened to them..."

"So the same things that make you good at your job," Rob affirmed.

"Huh?"

"Well, it's your questioning, your probing, your imagination that make you a great artist. Your ability to see the past isn't just supernatural, Taryn. You've always seen it in your mind, even before you could see it through the camera."

"Yeah, that's true," Taryn conceded, thinking of the many times she'd taken drives through the country, looking at old houses and tobacco barns and wondering about the people who once lived and worked in them.

"And now that same curiosity makes you curious about the ghosts. You can't cut it off. I bet you read Nancy Drew a lot as a kid," he teased her.

"Yeah, a little," Taryn smiled.

"And do you feel like this is just something in passing, something you can move on from, or is this one for you?" Rob asked. Matt had asked her almost the same exact thing.

"That's what I am trying to figure out."

Rob stood, patted her on top of her head, and walked to the small refrigerator in the corner. He offered her a drink and held his to his head. "Hotter than hell out there today," he muttered. "The fact is, you can't help all the ghosts. And not all ghosts want your help. Some can't be helped at all. You've got to learn and practice some control. Learn when to move forward, when to cut them off."

Taryn acquiesced. He was right. "Well, listen, I always seem to be coming to you for advice. Can I do something for you around here? I'm not in a big hurry to get back."

A slow grin spread across Rob's tanned face, making him look a decade younger. "As a matter of fact, I just got in a whole slew of books. You can alphabetize them, shelf them, and enter in the inventory. I'll take you to the store room..."

Taryn always left Rob with more than she went in with, and

not just in terms of advice. This time she left with new ear buds, a paper sack full of candles, and some essential oils he swore that, when mixed with a carrier oil, would help ease the pain in her joints. The narcotics didn't offer much relief but she hadn't tried eucalyptus oil yet...Who knew, though. It might work.

The restaurant was closed by the time she returned but she'd gone through a fast food place and picked up a sandwich and milkshake and she had snacks back in her room.

As it turned out, she'd done a little more shopping than she'd thought and her arms were full of paint supplies, clothes, and music CDs as she made her way up the walk to her lodgings. She thought she was balancing everything pretty well but as she was jiggling for her room key her cell phone flipped out of her pocket and landed on the floor with a crash.

"Well. Shit," Taryn muttered, peering over her bags to the floor. It was flipped open but at least it hadn't shattered. This was why she didn't own expensive electronics.

With her hands still full she carried the bags into the room and placed them up against the wall. Glad she left the lamp on while she was gone, the bedroom was filled with a cheerful glow now instead of being gloomy and uninviting.

Remembering her phone, Taryn turned around and started back out to the hallway. She stopped short, though, in the opening. The phone was no longer on the floor.

"What the hell?" Taryn asked, hands on her hips. Nobody was there. Nobody had come up behind her.

She was about to throw a little tantrum, convinced some phone thief had slipped up behind her and stolen her cheap Walmart phone, when something caught the corner of her eye. Her phone, now closed, was laying on the edge of her desk.

CHAPTER 9

*T*aryn wasn't usually up for breakfast but that

morning she woke up at 8:00 am, sharp, and feeling like her stomach was going to fall out if she didn't fill it soon.

Everyone else must have felt that way, too, because the dining room was crowded. When Jenny, the hostess, asked her if she minded sharing a table with someone else she swore it wasn't a problem. Of course, that "someone else" wound up being Andy, the nonbeliever book writer.

"Hey, I'm sorry about being rude the other day," Taryn apologized as soon as she was seated. "Working alone, not getting out much except to work, can kind of make you antisocial after awhile."

"No worries, my dear," Andy boomed. "I can get a little rude myself."

Taryn ordered her breakfast and then sat back awkwardly, not really knowing what to say. Andy appeared uneasy, too, so the two sat together quietly, trying to look interested in other things. Finally, she broke the silence.

"You're here pretty early," she observed with polite interest.

"Having some work done on my house," Andy explained. His glasses were fogging up and she couldn't understand it, though it fascinated her. It looked like little clouds were forming under the glass and she just could not look away. "Thought I'd stay here a few nights and get some relief from all the dust and hammering."

"It's a good place to get some peace," she chattered brightly. "Pretty, people friendly, good food. I've enjoyed being here."

"Yeah, well, they pay for you to stay here. I'm paying the regular tourist rate so I don't get much of a vacation," he stated with pronounced bitterness.

Taryn smiled uneasily, not knowing how to respond. She wasn't going to apologize for working. The food and lodging was part of her salary and she could go months without working at all.

"Well, it's a working vacation for me," she responded at last.

"You'd think they'd be able to find someone around here who could paint a picture," he mused. "So they wouldn't have to pay someone to stay here and eat."

What could she possibly say in response to that? If she agreed it was going to sound like she didn't think she should've been hired. But to say anything else would be argumentative. She just decided to let it go. Luckily the food arrived soon after.

They weren't but a few minutes into their meals, however, when Andy began ruminating again. "So you don't really believe that ghost nonsense do you?"

"Yes," she stated without apology. "I do."

Andy laughed, an unattractive sound coming from him. "Really?"

She concurred, unperturbed.

"But you went to college didn't you? Don't you have a degree?"

Taryn studied him with interest over her fresh fruit. "Yeah. I did. But what does that have to do with it? You know there are degree programs out there that study mythology, paranormal studies, religious experience, cultural anthropology, folklore..."

"Yes, but from a scientific viewpoint for the most part. In an observation kind of way. I think most intellectually evolved people these days wouldn't be giving in to supernatural explanations when science is reason," he argued.

"And yet you're writing a book on the Shakers?"

"But not because I believe in what they experienced," he stated. "I'm writing about the opposite."

It was no wonder they weren't paying him to stay there. She kept this thought to herself. It would go over like a lead balloon.

"Do you go to church?" he pressed. "Have you been baptized, saved?"

"Am I washed in the blood of the lamb?" she asked mildly. "No. I'm not religious. I don't subscribe to any one particular faith. But I believe in something and I respect those who do, as long as they don't go out of their way to press their beliefs on me."

"Some would say that's hypocritical, that you can't straddle both sides of the fence," he remarked.

"I'm not so concerned with what others think. All I can worry about is myself."

"So how much money do you make at things like this?" he asked, changing the subject.

"Not as much as I really need, but enough to get by," she replied. Taryn had always thought it was rude to talk of politics, money, or religion with someone she didn't know. He'd almost covered all three.

"So you're doing this until...until what?" he pressed. "What's the ultimate goal? You know, what kind of job are you waiting for?"

Taryn was confused. "What do you mean?"

"Well, artists can't *really* make a career out of painting. Not unless you're teaching or finding another way of supplementing your income," he replied primly.

It was difficult for people to see what she did as a real job, with a bonafide income. Taryn imagined it was that way with any freelancing business.

"I manage okay," she said simply.

"But back to these ghosts," he continued. "It's clear to see what's really going on."

"Yes?"

"Well," he rubbed his hands together, as though excited. "Let's say someone sees an apparition in a costume. It's a ghost! They've time traveled! Whatever. It's obvious they've just caught a glimpse of a docent or employee. And as for the person disappearing or being able to see through them? A trick of the light maybe. The mind sees what it wants to see."

"And the noises? The singing, the laughing, the talking when nobody's there?" Taryn asked, fascinated.

"Old pipes, the wind carrying voices from the other side of the park, people in another room..." he supplied, obviously quite pleased with himself.

"What about the people who wake up in the middle of the night and see a ghost in the room with them?"

"Dreaming, of course. Maybe a night terror, sleep paralysis. The power of suggestion because they've already come here believing the place is haunted."

Andy leaned back in the chair, causing it to creak just a little, and drummed his thick fingers on his ample stomach.

"I guess you have it all figured out then," Taryn mumbled wryly. She stood up and grabbed her knapsack. "I hope you have a good stay here and get lots of research done."

And I hope you get an eye full in the archive room, she thought to herself as she sauntered out of the busy dining room.

She might have been avoiding the archive room, but that

didn't mean she had to stop researching. She was going to get to the bottom of the mystery, no matter what. It seemed clear to her that whoever was haunting the park liked her (why else put out the fire and rescue her cell phone) and probably died a violent death there. Taryn thought it was the young woman she saw from her window and that maybe she'd been attacked and killed, either in the archive room or schoolhouse. She didn't know how the Shaker Town murder fit into the scheme of things, or if it did at all. Neither Rob nor Julie could be certain the elder who was murdered was male or female, or what decade it had happened in.

None of this gave Taryn much to work with. Still, the Shakers had been excellent record keepers and many of them kept diaries and letters they'd saved. There was a very good chance that she'd find a clue somewhere.

She also knew she wasn't asking the right person. Someone had to know more.

It took her three days and being a lot more social than she was used to but she finally found her man in Eddie Jay, resident horse wrangler.

Eddie Jay, who went by both names, was in his early sixties and had worked at Shaker Town for more than twenty years.

"I figure I know just about any time somebody farts around here," he bragged to Taryn. Incidentally, that's what everyone else had told her about him, too. He sounded perfect.

Taryn followed him around the barn, like a little kid, as he fed and brushed down the horses. They were big, beautiful beasts. She'd thought they were Clydesdale at first but he'd taken the time to explain to her that they weren't. And then he'd given her the long-running story on their history and how he was certain that the Budweiser horses weren't true Clydesdale, either. Taryn was itching to get on one of the horses and ride but her orthopedist back in Nashville had told her that with her Ehlers-Danlos Syndrome it could seriously injure her hip or back. She wasn't sure how hard she was going to take that advice yet.

"So you must know a whole lot about the history of the place," Taryn maintained, encouraging him to speak further. It didn't take much to get him talking, though; she'd already learned that.

"Oh yes. Know just about everything there is to know about this place here," he agreed. Unlike most of the other employees, he didn't wear a costume but his tattered jeans and short-sleeved flannel shirt were a different kind of uniform. She hadn't seen him wear anything else since she'd been there.

"So I was kind of wondering about the guy who was killed here, back in the 1800's," she added, just in case there was more than one.

"Uh huh, yep," he smacked his lips, a dry sound that made one of the horses shake his tail with vigor. "Hit aside of the head with something. Lived a few days before passing on. Never able to talk, though."

"So they don't know who did it?"

"Naw. Most likely someone from town come in and done it, trying to steal something. There was some lean winters around here, some folks didn't have much. Lots of jealousy of the people up here. They might have thought 'em quacks but when their food supply was low and their feet was cold they'd come a runnin," he grinned.

"So maybe somebody wanting something and they got caught?" Taryn pressed.

"Yeah, I'd say they got caught in the act and then clobbered the feller to keep him from blabbin.' They didn't take kindly to thieves back then," he added.

"There was a girl here about that time, too," Taryn badgered him, thinking of her ghost. "Maybe she was murdered, too. Or killed herself?"

Eddie Jay scratched the stubble at his chin and then ran his hand through his gray, but thick, head of hair. He considered her question as he studied the goats in the pen, like they might have the answer. Finally, he shrugged. "No, don't know of any woman dying. Leastways, not of anything unnatural. Maybe sickness or something. Ought to be in the record books, though."

"A suicide maybe?" she offered.

"Well, those happened, of course, but they weren't talked about. Wait a minute, are you talking about the white lady?"

Taryn nodded.

"Yeah, I seen her once. Kind of skipping around. Don't know who she is, though. Awfully young. I'd say she was somebody who got the lung fever. It happened."

Taryn was relieved to be speaking to someone who took ghosts in a matter-of-fact manner.

After thanking him for his time and giving both horses a quick petting, she started out of the barn and then stopped. "Hey, one more thing. Have you heard anything about babies in the pond?"

Eddie Jay snorted. "That's horse shit. They'd a been more likely to be pulling them out of the pond, not throwing them in. The more the merrier."

Looking at the schoolhouse now, it was hard to imagine that it had ever resembled the sound structure in her photographs. Each time she stood before it, however, she couldn't help but see the young woman running towards it and disappearing into its walls. As she painted, she let her mind create a story. It was not only a way of entertaining herself while she painted and listened to Jason Isbell sing "Alabama Pines," it was a way to see the building as something it used to be, so that it would hopefully comes across through her painting.

A little girl grew up here at Pleasant Hill, taken in by the Shakers because she was an abandoned orphan. She grew up following strict rules, like not talking during meal times, and never knowing the love of just one mother. But she had a good childhood, too; one that let her get an education in the summertime and run through the fields when nobody was looking. She had plenty to eat, a warm bed to sleep in at night, and an extended family larger than most children her age. Her life was regimented, but secure. She was always safe.

The schoolhouse was her favorite place. There, she learned not only scripture but how to write, how to put her thoughts on paper. She learned where different places on the map were, how the animals in nature differed from one another. The schoolhouse was her favorite place in the whole world and she looked forward to the days when she could sit at the uncomfortable desk and listen to her teacher talk about all the wonderful things she never knew existed. And sometimes there were children from the other world who came, too. The world's people. She was just as curious about them as she was the bullfrog or the oxen.

The little girl grew up and, as an adult, took the oath to become a Shaker herself. She had that choice, after all, and could've chosen to leave the village. But why? It was all she knew. Although she was schooled in herbs, in care, in meal making, in laundry and dyeing and spinning and was a little good in all those things, she was still drawn to the schoolhouse. So she became a teacher herself.

Each morning she would walk through the damp fog, excited about the day ahead. Maybe she would hum a little tune to herself as she crossed through the cold grass, the spider webs catching her ankles and the cattle calling in the distance. She'd make sure the desks were arranged properly, that her lessons were ready. She was happy and content that she had a calling she loved, and was allowed to do it.

The schoolhouse took on a cheerful appearance now, as Taryn painted. It was no longer the depressing ruins. Taryn could see the children filing in, some orderly and some not so much. She could hear cheerful chatter ringing out the windows, the sound of a soft but stern voice telling everyone to take their seats. As she tuned out the voices of the tourists around her, and the occasional ringing of the bell that signaled events and programs, she could sometimes hear the recitations, simple songs, and laughter.

This was a happy place.

The woman had been happy. She'd danced across the lawn, singing. She'd smiled. Surrounded by many, she was still alone in the world, but she was happy. Taryn could understand this.

It had all ended, though, and abruptly. Did another member attack her? Perhaps she'd been in the archive room, or whatever it was back then. A Shaker brother, or maybe even an outsider since the Shakers did do business with the people in the surrounding communities, came in on her. He'd been struck by her beauty, her innocence. Had come on to her. Maybe been angered by her refusal, her piousness. So he'd what, raped her? Killed her?

And then what? Her death was covered up? She'd been completely forgotten about over the years?

It wasn't a nice story but it was one that made a certain amount of sense. Her spirit was awfully happy, though, to have been brutally attacked and killed. That didn't make sense so much.

And Taryn couldn't forget the fact that when her fire had started, the shadowy figure had definitely been that of a man, not a petite woman.

The schoolhouse looked back at her expectantly. She could all but see it nod its nonexistent head in encouragement. She was on to *something*. She just wasn't sure *what*, yet.

CHAPTER 10

*T*he pond spread out before Taryn like a sheet of glass.

The day was overcast, the sky slate gray. It was reflected on the water's surface, making it opaque. Taryn couldn't paint outside, since the threat of rain was so great and sprinkles kept escaping, so she was using the day to answer emails, research, and balance her checkbook. The business end to what she did was soul crushing. She wished she could hire a Virtual Assistant, or at least a bookkeeper, but so far her budget would allow her neither.

When she needed a break she found herself down at the pond, perched on a wrought-iron bench, staring at the water. She tried to imagine Shakers stealing down to the water in the darkness, throwing children in it, but the image was at once so horrifying and funny in an ironic way that she didn't dwell on it. They were a peaceful people; they weren't murderers.

Her solitude was soon threatened by an old woman wearing pink polyester pants and a George Strait T-shirt. She looked to be at least eighty but moved with the grace of a teenager, her tiny feet barely touching the ground.

"You mind if I sit with you?" she gestured to the space next to Taryn. Her voice was strong and crisp.

"Sure, I'll share," Taryn replied, moving over to make more room. "Kind of a dreary day out today."

The woman, whose name tag read "Della," patted her blue-tinted hair. "Well, it's a little ugly but every day I actually wake up is a pretty good one to me. The first thing I do every morning before I even get out of bed is move all the body parts. If something hurts then I know I didn't go to heaven in the middle of the night so I know it's okay to get up and make a pot of coffee."

Taryn, who had also started doing a little of the same, laughed. "I always move all my joints, to see which one is going to hurt the worst that day. I don't care which one it is, but I like knowing in advance."

"That a girl," Della patted her in approval. "Get a grasp of the situation before moving forward."

That was some advice Taryn could apply to most areas of her life.

"Are you here with a tour group?" she asked politely.

Della snorted. "Yes. Something my daughter-in-law signed me up for. Said I needed to get out more. I wanted to do that damn bike ride up here. You know, the Bike to Shakertown event? But my son said I was too old, might fall over in the road. They signed me up with this group as a consolation prize."

"Are you having fun at least?"

Della shrugged, George's face moving up and down with her arms. "The park's nice but everyone in my group is just so damn old. They move slower than Christmas and we have to keep stopping so someone can pee."

This was positively the most fun Taryn had had in a long time.

"So what are you doing here? Are you hiding, too?" she asked Taryn, peering at her from the corner of her eye.

"I guess I am, in a way," Taryn replied. "But mostly hiding from work, from bills, from having to do things I need to do."

"Those are the best things to hide from," Della concurred with approval. "But always the hardest. They find you, sooner or later."

The two women sat in companionable silence for a few minutes, both watching the water. It was as still as a painting, as though it was waiting. For something.

"I come here sometimes, with my family, you know?" Della whispered softly. "I know it's just a pond and you can see those anywhere, but something about it always drags me back."

"I like the water myself," Taryn agreed. "I think it's from growing up in a city that was so far removed from the ocean. And maybe because I'm a Pisces."

"So am I," Della grinned. "Great minds and all. There's a sadness here, though. I've never been able to put my finger on it."

"It's meant to be haunted," Taryn explained. "I've just been sitting here thinking about that."

"Oh, the baby story. Or babies, I imagine. Yes, I've heard that as well."

"I don't think it's true," Taryn vowed with passion. "I don't think they would've done that. Sometimes those stories float around and we forget how they started in the first place."

"Maybe," Della agreed. "But I stayed here one night. Oh, it was years and years ago. Couldn't sleep so I came down here for a little walk. Slipped and fell on my way back up and nearly broke my damned leg. But anyway. I saw something here. Not a baby but a man. It was most certainly a man. He stood watching the water for the longest time. I sat right here on the bench, so I wouldn't disturb him," Della motioned to the seat. "Looked like he had more on his mind than I did, which was just indigestion."

"What happened?"

"His troubles were a lot more than I'd originally thought," Della laughed a little. "After a few minutes he turned around and faded right into the night. He wasn't real."

"I know this is going to sound funny," Taryn began, "but did you feel anything when he was here? I mean, were you afraid? Was it good energy, bad?"

"I know what you're asking and the answer is that I felt nothing but sadness for the poor fellow. He wasn't there to hurt me, or to hurt anyone. Just thinking, being alone. Kind of like we are now."

"I think this park is full of ghosts," Taryn blurted. She was thinking about the fire in her room and the male presence that had snuffed it out. Was it the same spirit? Or was the park just overrun with them, none of them connected?

"Yes, it is. Lots of heartache here, lots of sadness. Lots of happiness, too, but any time you get that much passion in a place, released or not, it's going to leave something behind," Della smiled again, but she looked tired.

A shrill voice cut through the air behind them and Taryn turned to see a stocky woman in khaki shorts and a red, V-neck sleeveless top inching down the incline towards them. "Susan, Susan!" she called. "I thought I'd lost you!"

"Well, guess it's time to go back," Della sighed with a mixture of regret and irritation. "It was nice talking to you."

"But your name tag says..." Taryn gestured in confusion.

She snorted. "I like to mess with them sometimes. When you get to be my age and have lived with yourself long enough sometimes it's nice to try on someone else's skin."

Taryn had just slid into the driver's seat when her phone went off. It was Rob.

"Did I screw up the alphabetizing?" she asked, only half joking. "You know I still have to sing the song to remember what order the letters come in, especially around 'P.'"

"Ha! You did fine," he assured her. "I'm calling because I found something for you and I thought you might be interested."

Taryn was anxious to get on the road, she was hungry and craving something really bad for her. She waited. The last thing she needed to do was run the car off the road while she talked. "Yeah? What did you find?"

"Two things, actually. One is a book of ghost stories about the Shakers. I think you'll like it. The other is an old research piece, a bunch of letters and journal entries. I don't think these are the kinds of things you're going to find at the gift shop there," he laughed.

"Where did you find them?" she asked.

"I have my ways. Anyhow, I can stick them in the mail if you'd like. Should get there the day after tomorrow."

Taryn bit her lip nervously. If they were important to him she didn't want to be responsible for something happening. "You sure you don't mind parting with them?"

"Oh, hell no. You're fine. Just send 'em back when you're done!"

Of course, it was highly likely that she'd already read the letters and journal entries; she had been spending a lot of time in the archives. But the ghost stories would be fun and, who knew, something might jog her memory.

Harrordsburg had an array of restaurants to choose from and she needed a break from the dining room at the park. Matt would be appalled at her turning her nose up at garden-fresh vegetables for a McChicken but there was only so much healthy food a body could take. Her doctors had all encouraged her to eat an anti-inflammatory diet to help cut down on the inflammation and pain from her EDS, and she tried to stick to it as much as possible, but living didn't seem like it would be very fun if she didn't occasionally splurge and eat something that would survive a nuclear attack.

The scenic country drive to Harrodsburg took her past small farms, green misty fields, and beautiful old stone fences. She stopped and pulled over once to take a picture of an old house that looked as though it had been abandoned for many years. Nature had taken over and was slowly choking the walls to death with ivy and honeysuckle not yet bloomed. She could barely make out the windows, with just a tiny sliver of glass poking courageously through the greenery. The front door was standing wide open, an invitation for travelers, and a broken wooden chair sat on the front porch and stared at the main road, waiting for visitors who never came.

Taryn got back in her car and began driving again, feeling sad. As much as she adored the old houses and found her passion in envisioning the past, sometimes the sadness was just too much to take. When she saw an abandoned structure falling apart like that she didn't just see boards, a collapsed roof, and broken window panes. Instead, she saw a happy family standing in front of it, proud to call it home. She saw the mother standing in the hot kitchen clanging pans, the smells of chicken and apple cobbler drifting through the house. She saw small children lying on a rag rug in the living room foyer, bickering with one another or playing. She saw a man coming home from work, stopping on the steps and smiling as he listened to the sounds drifting out: This was his family and where he lived.

Every old, abandoned house had once been someone's home, had once held dreams and hopes. She believed these places had feelings, almost as much as people did.

Miss Dixie afforded her the opportunity to see the past like most people could never imagine. But sometimes that past was just too much, even the good parts. Taryn felt an almost unbearable responsibility towards the churches, the houses, the schools, the tobacco barns...Like she wasn't trying hard enough to save them all.

In the end, Taryn ended up not at a chain with burgers but at a small-town diner, eating the same kind of food she'd most likely have had at the park. Still, it was a change of scenery.

The restaurant, called "Evelyn'", looked like the inside of an old woman's purse had exploded. The walls were ensconced with pictures of flowers, lighthouses, and horses. Shelves containing angel statues, more lighthouses, and collections of salt 'n pepper shakers were scattered throughout the room. Each table held a cheap Dollar General vase full of plastic flowers, squarely atop an intricate doily.

It smelled wonderful.

The wait staff all looked matronly with ample bosoms and waistlines, another good sign for the quality of food. Taryn didn't always trust food prepared by teenagers who would rather be anywhere else. Her waitress' name was Sandra, at least according to her name tag, and when she smiled she revealed a missing front tooth. She probably weighed over three-hundred pounds but could dance around the tables holding heavy trays of food as good as any ballerina.

After Taryn ordered a dinner of salmon patties, macaroni and tomato juice, mashed potatoes, and cornbread muffins she sat back and observed the room again. It was full to capacity, mostly older couples who chewed their food slowly and didn't look at each other. Above Taryn's head was a faded black and white photograph of an elderly woman with shockingly white hair, a floral-print dress, and thick glasses. She smiled a sweet smile and leaned up against a fence post, her hands crossed primly in front of her. It was the only photo of a person.

"That's Evelyn," Sandra supplied when she returned with a plate of deviled eggs. "She's the owner's great grandmother."

"Oh, that's nice," Taryn smiled. "Was she known for her cooking?"

"She was known for everything," Sandra laughed. "She cooked for the old one-room schoolhouse here in town for a long time. Then her husband opened a hardware store and she helped him run it. Had eleven kids, if you can imagine. They all lived in top of the store over there." Sandra gestured out the window to a building across the street. It was now a dry cleaner's on one side and a flea market on the other.

The food was delicious and Taryn ate every bite. Then she ordered butterscotch pie and took it to go. She'd be hungry again later.

An elderly woman rang her up at the antiquated cash register and Taryn waited patiently as she hunted and pecked for all the numbers. "You from here?" she asked with a grunt.

"No, just here working," Taryn supplied.

"You in some kind of medical supplies?"

Taryn was taken by surprise. Nobody'd ever asked her that before. "Um, no, I'm a painter. I'm working up at Shaker Village."

"Oh, yeah," the woman bobbed her head. With one last grunt she hit a button and the drawer sprung open. Taryn handed her the cash and she began the slow process of counting out the change. "Lots of people come here for that. My great-granny was a Shaker. That's her, there," she gestured to the picture above Taryn's table.

"Evelyn?" Taryn asked.

"Yes, that's her. Joined up with her family when she was a little thing. Turned eighteen and went through the whole ordeal of becoming a real Shaker, cause they won't let you do that any sooner, and then took off about a year later. Don't know why but glad she did. I wouldn't be here if she'd stayed."

"Where'd she go?" Taryn asked with interest.

"Here in town," the woman shrugged. "Had some cousins here and stayed with them. Her little brother, my great uncle, came with her eventually. He went on to become a judge."

"What year would that have been?"

"Oh, I guess around 1855. Bad days for folks here in Kentucky. Lots of people joining the Shakers then, lots of people leaving, all for the same reason."

"The war," Taryn murmured.

"Yep, that's right."

The Shakers were pacifists so they received exemption from military duty. They'd even approached President Lincoln in the Civil War with a petition for exemption from the military draft. It had been granted.

Taryn thought she was finished talking but just as she started to thank her and say goodbye, the woman gave a watery cough and then started up again. "Yeah, that's my great-granny Evelyn. And my great uncle, Junior. Charles was his real name, of course. Rogers, they were. Last name Rogers. Reckon once they left they never saw their parents again. Strange thing about those folks."

Taryn signaled her agreement. "Yeah, they had some interesting ways of doing things.

"Would've been a sight, though, to have seen them doing their singing and dancing. Folks from around here used to go and watch them for hours making fools of themselves. The women dancing around like they was little kids and the men jumping and yelling. They didn't have the movies and the video games back then, see," she muttered in distaste. "You had to be entertained in other ways."

Taryn suppressed the urge to giggle.

"Anyway, I hope you enjoy your stay. Come back and see us again."

Taryn thanked her and walked back to her car, the heat still wafting up from the pavement even though the sun was set.

CHAPTER 11

*U*sing what she knew about the Shakers, Taryn sat

down

at her desk and attempted to make a chart, using the people she knew about and what she'd already seen. So far, she knew an elder had been murdered.

Although there were elders and eldresses in the different Shaker communities, there were actually four who oversaw the whole thing. They lived in New York and were called the "Central Ministry." All the societies had ministers and these trained the neophytes went out into the world beyond the Shakers to preach and find new members.

Within the smaller communities there were different groups called "families" and these also had two elders and eldresses. Two of each, who were in charge of their spiritual life and well-being. Families also had Deacons and Deaconesses and these guys oversaw the crafts, farm work and stuff. The Trustees, on the other hand, oversaw the legal things and business side of the Families. It was hard to say, without looking at the records, who the elder truly was. He could've been a legitimate elder, or he could've been a Deacon or Trustee and over the years the identity was confused. She hoped Rob's book would help with this. She was still trying to avoid the archive room, thanks to Andy.

It was highly possible that the elder could've been killed by an outsider. Not only did the Shakers do business with them, but once their population started declining and they didn't have as many men around they needed to hire out. The hired hands chopped wood, stacked hay, and did other odd jobs. They were usually paid every day and it was good money if you could get hired on and didn't mind not being able to talk to the women.

Money seemed to be high on the list of motives when it came to murder, with love (or jealousy) right behind. She'd stick to those two motives for now.

When her phone rang Taryn answered it absently. She was stuck when her aunt's attorney began talking on the other end.

'Taryn? I hope I haven't caught you at a bad time," he apologized. He always sounded so flustered, like he'd been caught doing something he wasn't supposed to.

"I'm fine. Everything okay?"

Taryn's Aunt Sarah had passed away back in the fall, a fact Taryn was still trying to deal with every day. Although she hadn't seen her aunt in years, she'd always been someone Taryn had admired from afar; indeed, she was one of the few adults who had treated Taryn with love and respect. As the only surviving relative (Sarah had never married or had children), Taryn inherited her estate in New Hampshire.

"It's fine, it's fine. I checked on the house today and everything looks good. I was wondering, however, if you planned on coming up here soon?"

Taryn let out a deep breath. She'd been avoiding that so far, the idea of going through Sarah's belongings and walking through the rooms of that old farmhouse without her just felt too much. Taryn had already lost her parents, her grandmother, her fiancé (or husband, depending on who she was talking to). If she lost Matt she would truly be all alone in the world; she had nobody left.

"I am hoping to come up this summer," she replied. "I'm on a job at the moment and can't leave."

"Well, my advice is to hire a manager or overseer to keep an eye on it," he lectured. "Nobody's vandalized it, yet, but it's a big house in a remote area. People are going to start getting curious."

Taryn felt a moment of panic. She certainly didn't have the money to hire anyone. She even did her own taxes and hoped the IRS had a sense of humor.

As though reading her mind, the attorney laughed. "I know someone and can send you their information. Your aunt didn't leave behind a fortune, but you'll have enough to get someone for a few months and still have a nice sum left over."

Taryn let of a sigh of relief. Well, that didn't sound so bad.

"Okay, that's good. If you can just email me then I'll get in touch with them."

She hung up the phone feeling a little depressed, her Shaker ghosts and drama momentarily put to the side.

"Sorry I'm late," Julie sang as she arranged bottles of spirits on the small table. She was set up outside, since the weather was nice, and a couple of guys cleared room for the musicians who would be showing up later. "All kinds of hoopla in my neighborhood and I'm too nosy not to get involved in that."

"What happened?" Taryn asked from the table next to her. She wasn't super hungry, but an appetizer plate of fried green tomatoes (one of the South's most reverent offerings) hit the spot.

"Someone broke into the house next door. It's being built, you know? Anyway, they went in and sold the copper and stuff. Been happening a lot lately," Julie confided.

"I heard about that. Any idea who's doing it?"

"Not a clue. But it's not just here. You hear about it in Danville, Lexington, Richmond..." Julie let her voice trail off as she ducked under the table to retrieve a runaway cup. "It freaks me out a little, though, because I live alone. Knowing that there were burglars next door doesn't put my soul at ease."

"Well, maybe it means they've hit your area now and are going to move on to someplace else," Taryn suggested weakly. She would've felt the same way.

"You know, I kinda feel bad for the crooks, too. Not a lot of jobs around here and people are desperate. Not just because they're druggies but because they got bills to pay."

Taryn acquiesced. She often felt financially desperate herself. Before the Shaker Town job came along she was on the tip of accepting a job from a company that wanted her to paint a series of chain bar and grills for them to hang in their entrances.

Taryn finished her meal but then sat back, intent on listening to the band. They had a little bit of a heavy metal bluegrass sound to them, "metal grass" or "punk grass" some people called them, and they were good. She wished she'd left sooner, though, when she saw Andy stalking up to her table.

"You mind if I sit here?" he asked prissily.

Taryn shrugged and moved her plate over to make room for him. He looked out of breath and out of patience.

"You okay?" she asked.

"I have to stay here at least two more nights," he huffed. We've had a water leak at the house and have to replace some pipes. No telling what that's going to cost me."

"We were just talking about money," Taryn said, gesturing to Julie. Julie was busy laughing with a small group of German tourists as they pointed at the American beers on display and scratched their heads. They wouldn't find much comparison to what they were used to.

"So how's the work going?" she asked. She didn't care for the man but he was all she had at the moment.

"Fine, fine," he answered with a wave of his hand. "I was knee deep in records today.

"Yeah? What did you find?"

"Mostly school stuff," he shrugged. "They seemed to have a hard time keeping a teacher towards the end of the nineteenth century. Just one right after another."

Taryn's ears perked up. That was, after all, her area. "What happened?"

"I don't know," he shrugged. "Work too hard, maybe. Lots of women leaving. Like that one who the restaurant was named after."

"Evelyn's?" Taryn asked in surprise.

"That's the one. She was a schoolteacher here for, oh, I guess four years. That was the longest stretch I found."

Taryn leaned back in her chair and considered. The band was playing a low-key version of the Avett Brothers' "I and Love and You" and the air was damp, but warm. It suddenly didn't seem so bad sitting out there, even with her current company.

"I met her great granddaughter when I ate there a few nights ago," Taryn volunteered. "She talked a little about her living here, but didn't say anything about her being a teacher. I'm painting the school at the moment."

"Well, she was there. Life just seems like a series of coincidences sometimes," he said bitterly and then took a drink of his beer. Taryn still had to laugh at the irony of drinking alcohol at Shaker Town.

"Know anything about the murder here?" she asked hopefully.

"Nah. Probably fell and hit his head on something and wasn't even killed at all."

"So I was thinking..." Taryn paced around her room, getting ready for bed, and kept Matt on speakerphone.

"Yep?"

"You could come up here and we could drink wine and then have sex in my room. We could even walk up the same stairs together. You know, just break all the rules?"

"You could get pregnant, too, and we could throw procreation in there. It would be very un-Shaker of you," Matt added.

Taryn stopped in her tracks, her shirt and arms raised over her head. He was joking, right? "You're joking, right?" she asked, edging closer to the phone.

"Mostly. I'm getting older, though, and think about having kids sometimes. Don't you?"

Taryn balanced herself on the edge of the bed while she pulled on her pajama bottoms. "In theory I guess. But it seems a little impractical to me, seeing as to how I am not married, don't have any form of stable income, and have some health issues."

"The health problems would be concerning," Matt agreed. "But we could take care of the other things. In fact, when I checked my mail today I saw I had a coupon for one of the jewelry stores in the mall. I think it might have been a sign."

The idea of Matt proposing was both thrilling and a little unsettling. "Matt, please don't buy me an engagement ring from the mall using a coupon."

"Why?" he asked, sounding genuinely puzzled.

"Never mind."

Since they hadn't seen each other in awhile and she was in a pretty good mood Taryn considered flashing herself in her bra and sending him a picture but it was unlikely he'd appreciate that. Matt belonged in another century and would probably go around wearing a top hat if he could find a good, inexpensive supply of them. And there was always the chance it could go viral. She could see the memes being created already...

Still in a happy mood, Taryn crawled under the covers and flipped on the television. Her favorite episode of *Designing Women* (Bernice's sanity hearing) was on and Taryn snuggled under the thick, cool duvet and smiled. Life wasn't so bad at the moment. As her feet dug into the coolness of the cotton sheet below her, she smiled and felt a momentary surge of euphoria.

It was almost immediately replaced by a sharp, sudden tug of sadness. The despair hit her like a ton of bricks, starting at her forehead and moving in a luxurious wave down her body to her stomach, where it settled. The feeling of hopelessness, lonesomeness, and grief were not unfamiliar to her; she'd been having similar incidents since she was a child. Life felt futile, pointless, and she was divided between wanting to burst into tears and feeling so numb she couldn't move.

The feeling only lasted for a couple of minutes and then it was gone, leaving behind only a little residue as a reminder. Feeling neither bliss nor depression now she turned back to the television and tried to watch.

The pain was searing. It cut through her like a knife, ripping apart her insides. She'd never known such torture. She wanted to babble, to cry out, to lose her eyes and just disappear. It consumed her with a heaviness, though, and was relentless.

She, who was Taryn and yet wasn't, looked around in a blind panic. It was dark outside and the ground beneath her was wet from the early-evening rain. She was alone.

She tried to focus on the tree line, the building behind her, the sounds of the crickets and tree frogs, but the pain ate at her. She was inside of it, unable to see or make sense of the world around her.

And yet while it burned and stabbed and ripped, she thought about him, about the act he'd committed on her. She felt him grasping her legs again, gouging her breasts until they were sore and tender. The aching spot on her head where he'd pulled a clump of hair out and then casually balled it in his fist while he pummeled her. The blood she drew from biting down on her lip. It was bitter and acidic, like early-summer tomatoes.

She cried for that, too.

CHAPTER 12

*T*aryn spent the next morning sore in a way that

wasn't EDS related. Her lower back, groin, and thighs ached and she felt violated. The dream from the night before still made her shudder. Like some of the others, it hadn't felt like a dream at all. She'd finally woke up in relief, happy to be back in her room with the television on. She'd even sent Matt a quick text ("bad dream, wish I could see you") and then sat in the middle of her bed, phone in hand, hoping he'd write back. It was late, though, and he wasn't up. She'd not been able to go back to sleep so she simply stayed up and worked.

There was no doubt in her mind that the woman she continued to see had been sexually assaulted. As a woman she knew what it was like to say no and not have it taken seriously. She knew the irrational guilt of making the man feel angry and frustrated. Taryn, herself, had given in on more than one occasion simply because she couldn't handle the inner turmoil of having someone angry or upset. And there had been some of that in her dream.

The woman might not have put up the fight some might expect now, but she'd been violated all the same.

How awful it must have been for her, Taryn thought, to have been physically hurt in such a manner. And then there was the psychological factor. Shakers believed it was their celibacy that would help them achieve their place in the afterlife.

She technically had one more week there at the park and knew she'd be finished by then. Her job was to paint but she planned on using every free moment trying to figure out what the hell was going on.

The dining room at dinner was a flurry of activity. Not only was it crowded with the usual suspects, Andy was holding court in a corner, face red and hands on hips. Tourists and wait staff were crowded around him, heads nodding in sympathy.

Since Taryn was seated next to him there was little she could do but listen.

"It's going to cost me more money than I even care to think about," he fumed.

"What happened?" Taryn asked her server as she sat a glass of lemonade in front of her.

"Oh, his house is being worked on and last night someone broke in and stole the copper pipes. Police don't have a clue."

Well, Taryn could certainly understand his frustration. She'd be on the tear, too, if someone broke in and stole something of hers. Thievery was so...violating.

Once the drama settled down and the onlookers cleared away, Taryn turned around and addressed him. "I'm sorry about your house," she apologized. "Did they take anything else?"

"No, just the pipes," he sighed. "Looks like I'll be here a little longer. At least the management offered me a free room for the rest of the week. I'm almost as important as you now."

He continued to find ways of irritating her, just when she thought she could get used to him.

"Bad way to have to get it, though," she murmured.

"Yeah, well..."

Since she felt genuine remorse for him she thought it only right that he not wallow alone. "You want me to come and sit with you?"

He gestured towards the empty seat, neither rudely nor invitingly. Taryn gathered her utensils and glass and moved over. "How's the writing going?" she asked.

He shrugged, his large shoulders rumbling under his sports shirt. "I'll meet my deadline. Already making plans for a book tour next year," he added, a smug smile lighting up his face. She tried her best to look interested, if not overly impressed, and his face tightened. "So how's the painting?"

"It's going," she answered. "You never really know how these things are going until they're finished."

"Aren't these companies and people you work for worried you're going to take them for a ride?"

"What?" Taryn asked, genuinely bewildered. "What do you mean?"

153

"You know," he smiled. "You say it will take two months when you can really get it done in a week. Drag it out to get more money and incentives from the job."

"Um...I've never done that," Taryn replied, feeling a little ball of anger forming in the pit of her stomach. "But thanks for giving me the idea."

"You don't really hear about painters anymore, do you?" he mused. "I mean, the general population doesn't hear about the artists. Where are the Warhols? The Picassos? Even Grandma Moses? I guess it's because painting has become so accessible to everyone that it's not as special anymore."

Taryn glared at him.

"Oh, not to imply that *yours* isn't good. I'm sure it is," he added in haste.

She thought she might hit him. She felt like physically lashing out.

Luckily, he seemed to have finished his meal and was starting to collect his belongings. Now that the attention had died away, and Taryn wasn't appreciating his distress enough, it appeared he was ready to move on.

With a briefcase in his hand, papers sticking out at odd angles, he said his goodbyes to the people around him. Taryn thought he was about to walk off when he stopped and looked down at her. "I almost forgot," he began. "I found something you might like."

"Yeah?"

He placed the briefcase on the table and began rummaging through the mess. Finally, he plucked a single sheet of paper out and handed it to Taryn. "This is a copy of a very old photo of Evelyn, the old school teacher. Of course, she'd not so old here. I knew you were working on that history some and thought you might like it. You can keep this copy."

Taryn held the sheet in trembling fingers, not sure why she was so surprised. After all, she'd already looked into that face several times during her stay. She just hadn't expected her ghost to be so photogenic in person.

The trails that snaked around the Shaker village had been

calling Taryn since her arrival. She kept telling herself she was going to take a walk around them, but she always let it get too dark on her. Something had woken her up uncharacteristically early, though, and she was determined to get in a walk before breakfast. It promised to be a bright, sunny day and the fog from the nearby river was still clawing the ground. It would be burned off soon, but she liked the atmosphere and was itching to get out in it before it disappeared.

Miss Dixie had a fully charged battery and a blank SD card. She was ready to explore.

Since it was only a little after 7:00 am the only other people Taryn saw milling around were employees. They paid little notice of her as she strolled through the field, the grass wet with dew, and made her way to the path. It was chilly and she was glad she'd thrown on the sweatshirt, the Vanderbilt letters faded after many, many washings.

While she walked towards the tree line she hummed a little Springsteen, "Dancing in the Dark." It was her rock-out song and she liked the line about being tired of sitting around trying to write the book. She was not a writer herself but often tired of trying to paint and sketch, especially when the motivation was lacking.

After doing some research online and reading study after study Taryn had started trying some supplements for her medical problems. It meant taking a handful of multivitamins and supplements every day: potassium, magnesium, Vitamin B12, Vitamin B6, Vitamin C, and a probiotic. She'd also started trying hemp seed oil in tablet form. Something must have been working because not only was the pain in her back and legs more manageable, she felt like she was in a better mood as well. She'd always enjoyed going out for walks and over the past year it had been getting harder and harder. Feeling better, or at least a little better, meant a greater return of freedom for her.

When she turned the corner she left the airy, openness of the fields and traveled into the dark canopy of the forest. Little had changed since the Shakers lived there, although a lot of it had been cleared since then. Taryn loved the quietness of the trees and even when things were quiet, like now, she imagined she could hear them breathing. She believed that trees, like old houses, had their own kinds of souls. And they remembered, probably more than anything. Sometimes she liked to place her hands on the trunks and listen. People would probably have thought she was crazy if they could see her; well, except for Matt. He believed that as well. Matt, who didn't subscribe to any particular religion either, always maintained that the best kind of church was outside because that's where you could feel closest to the creator.

Up ahead, the trail dipped over the side of the hill. Taryn could hear water below and she followed the sound with interest. She had mixed feelings about water. She wasn't a great swimmer and was a little afraid of the water, and yet she was endlessly fascinated by it.

Today the river was muddy and fast. The rain from the days before had left it swollen and the thick, chocolate-brown water swirled past her choked with leaves, branches, and other debris. It moved at a dizzying pace and watching it made Taryn feel like she was moving along with it. She stumbled a little and feared of falling in headfirst, caught by the pace. Grabbing onto a nearby tree trunk for support, she lowered herself to the soft ground and sat. Bits of bright blue sky now peeked through the branches above her, leaving a dappled pattern over the earth. It was peaceful sitting there watching the water.

She felt rather than heard the presence behind her. It gathered strength slowly and inched towards her, a pulsating ball of power. The morning sky was blacked out now, a shadow covering the ground around her. She looked up through a veil of black, the outside world barely more than a shadow. The unknown force behind her inched closer and closer, cloaking itself around Taryn, squeezing her and kneading her skin until she was struggling to get out of its powerful grip. She was absorbing it, whatever it was, and could feel it pawing at her, trying to seep into her skin, her mind, her soul. The vengeance and need were there in its power, she could feel it. It wasn't just provoked, it was *aroused*.

She choked, coughed, and gagged from the slippery smoke that slithered past her gaping lips and crept down her throat. She writhed in place, kicking and waving her hands in self-defense, but it held onto her hard as it seductively slid under her sweatshirt and into her pants, clawing and scratching. There was no shape; this was no man or woman. The sheer terror brought tears to Taryn's eyes as she fought against it, trying to force it out of every fold and crevice.

And then something else appeared. Although it was also dark, she could see the opacity outside her veil, almost within reach. There was anger, and not just from her. As the mystifying shape dropped down on her she screamed but above that there was another sound, a bellowing, that made the leaves on the trees shake. In an instant, the thing that had consumed her was gone, vanishing as though it had never been there.

She was left whimpering, cold and dismayed. Still trembling in fear, she attempted to straighten her shirt and smooth back her hair but her arms and legs were weak and wouldn't stop shaking. She could barely move.

Something else was still with her. The other thing, the one that had fallen on her; it was beside her. It seemed to be waiting for something, observing. She was afraid to look and tried to inch away but when she made to move a pale hand reached out, alabaster stone, and grazed her knee. She had a hole in her pants and small drops of blackish blood leaked from a tiny wound. The hand touched her there and warmth flooded through her, like little rivers of fire. She stopped shaking. In less trepidation now she slowly turned and looked, the closeness of the thing jarring. But she didn't jump back in fear; it was a man she was looking at. His curly brown hair shone in the pale, filtered light; his eyes were tempered. He looked both at Taryn and *through* her at the same time. When she opened her mouth to speak, he disappeared.

CHAPTER 13

When all else failed, there was always Matt.

"I need help," Taryn spoke rapidly into the phone, trying to tell him as much as possible before he sunk into work.

"Okay, what can I do?" he asked reasonably. "You need some research? Some investigating?"

Despite the fact that Matt was not a naturally nosy person, unlike Taryn, he was very good at digging stuff up. He missed his calling as a reference librarian.

"Maybe. If I send you some information can you take a look?"

"Sure. What's going on?"

Taryn quickly filled him in on her dreams, the photo of Evelyn, and what transpired down at the river. "I know for sure now that there are three distinct spirits: the man, the evil thing, and the woman," she finished in a rush. "I think the man might be the protector, kind of the overseer of the park. He seems to want to protect me and probably others as well."

"So what are you aiming to do here?" Matt asked. "If he's a protector then he's a good thing to have around, right?"

"Well, yeah," Taryn admitted.

"And the woman?"

"I don't know. She just kind of dances around really," Taryn replied lamely. It sounded silly now.

"And the other thing? The 'evil thing'?"

"I guess I want to make that thing disappear," Taryn shuddered. "Nobody would want it hanging around, right?"

"Taryn," Matt began gently, "maybe there's nothing to be solved here. It sounds like they're going along on their daily business and all seem to be happy about doing it. Well, except for maybe the evil thing. Yet it's possible you're one of the few who can sense it. You are unnaturally sensitive, you know?"

He had a point and it while it should have been encouraging, it actually deflated her a little. "Well, what about the murder?" she asked at last. "What if the man I keep seeing is the elder who was killed? And the evil thing is the thing that killed him? Maybe I am meant to solve that..."

"And maybe not..."

"Matt, dammit, I am meant to be here," Taryn pronounced with more force than she'd meant to use. "I know it!"

"Okay, okay, calm down. I believe you. Send me names, dates, whatever you have and I'll try to check them out," he promised.

But part of the problem was that Taryn had almost nothing to go on, save for her own dreams and a couple of ghost sightings. For once she had almost zero clue of who the spirits could be or what they wanted.

She caught a break that evening when she ducked into the

dining room for dinner and saw a befuddled Julie trying to organize her bar. "Hey, Taryn!" she called, motioning her over. "I have something to tell you."

"Yeah? What's up?"

"I talked to my mom last night. Her family's been around Mercer County since, well, forever. Since there was a fort here. She knows a lot about the history. Really got into genealogy, too, when she retired."

Taryn leaned against the wall and sipped on a glass of ice water and marveled at the fact that Julie could carry on a conversation with her, set out what she needed, and mix drinks all at the same time. Taryn was having trouble multitasking these days herself.

"Find anything out?"

"Maybe," she confessed. "The guy who was murdered? His name was Morgan. He wasn't old like most people seem to think he was. Maybe forty? Anyway, Mom says that some people thought a Shaker killed him and that they just kind of covered it up. You know, dispense their own brand of justice?"

Taryn considered. "Makes sense." It would also fit with the man she'd seen in the forest. He could've been forty, although he looked younger. Well, maybe being dead for more than one hundred years did that to a person…It would explain, too, why he kept hanging around. He had a need for vengeance and felt like protecting everyone else, especially since he'd suffered such an awful fate.

"Hey Julie, have you ever seen a guy ghost here?" Taryn asked, realizing she hadn't talked about him yet.

"No, not that I can remember," Julie answered.

"Okay, well, what about someone helping you? Being, you know, kind of considerate?"

Julie grinned. "Is he good looking? Sounds like my kind of ghost. Seriously, though, I have heard of that but haven't seen it myself."

"Yeah? What happened?"

Julie wiped her hands on a bar towel and then walked over to Taryn. Everyone who was waiting to be seated, and taking a little pre-dinner spirit, had moved on. "It was to Dustin actually. He was here at Christmas, leading one of the tours in his wagon, and the horse skidded or tripped or something. Whatever horses do when they almost fall. Dustin said it could've been hurt real bad but then it was like, from out of nowhere, he saw the outline of a man's arm shoot out and actually steady the horse."

"Geeze," Taryn replied, envisioning the scene: tourists huddled together under blankets, the lanterns adorned with wreathes, snow falling in big fat flakes from the sky, and the beautiful horse stumbling.

"I think there was another time when he was working up on the roof of the barn and he lost his balance. Something reached out and grabbed him. Or something like that." Julie waved her hand in the air. "I can't really remember."

"Thanks for sharing that," Taryn said warmly. "I'm trying to put all these stories together to see what I can come up with."

Taryn ate her meal and then grabbed a drink outside while she listened to the band. It was a group of women playing that night and they had a folksy bluegrass sound that she loved.

She listened to them go through a repertoire of Patty Griffin and Lucinda Williams and then smoothly transition into early Alison Krauss.

Taryn wasn't meant to be drinking alcohol. She'd never been much of a drinker to start with, she didn't like feeling out of control if she could help it, but the progression of the EDS seemed to be affecting her brain more and more and even a drink or two these days made her feel loopy. It was usually followed by a day of increased pain and stomach sickness that reminded her of the flu—not fun. But the occasional drink was okay, especially if she hadn't taken any heavy pain meds that day.

Now the Bailey's was starting to go to her head, and in a nice way. The warmness seeped into her arms and legs, tingling her fingers and toes. She spotted Andy off in the distance and gave him a little wave; not even the sight of him could ruin her good mood. Her painting was looking fabulous, Carol had maintained as much earlier that afternoon, and this isolated, insulated place was a happy one. Well, when the ghosts were playing fair. The food was good, the accommodations comfortable, and she was well taken care of. She'd even become friendly with enough people that, while not necessarily friends, at least made her feel not as lonely.

The female lead, a willowy woman with a flat chest and stringy hair down to her waist, pulled out a banjo and stepped back up to the microphone. Her low voice carried out over the small crowd, the opening lines of Gillian Welch's "Orphan Girl."

Taryn straightened a little and smiled, singing along with the others when she got to the chorus. It was one of her favorite songs. There wasn't a bad track on that album and Taryn always made the time to see her and Dave when they were in Nashville.

But then Taryn stopped and let the melancholy lyrics wash over her. She had no mother or father either. No sister or brother. She, too, was an orphan girl by the very definition since her parents were dead. Completely alone in the world, other than Matt. He was her sole link to her own mortality, the only one who would really mourn her if she was gone.

Her thoughts fell to Evelyn then, and her younger brother. Evelyn had not been an orphan, at least when she arrived at Shaker Town. But why had she left and taken her sibling? What happened to her parents? Once they'd arrived at the village they'd ceased being her parents and, instead, became her brother and sister. She was an orphan girl, too.

Maybe, Taryn thought, that's why she likes me. *You can live among a hundred people and still feel very, very alone.*

CHAPTER 14

*T*aryn woke up feeling as excited as a kid at Christmas.

Melissa, a woman she'd met while working the job over in Vidalia at Windwood Farm, was coming to visit her at the park. Taryn had arranged to take the whole day off, which was fine since her work was a day ahead of schedule. She'd stayed up most of the night before working on it and in a few days it would be completed. She'd have to move on then, of course, and wasn't yet sure where that was going to be to, but she wasn't going to worry about that just yet. The money she'd earned at Shaker Town would see her through for another month or two until she found something else.

Since it was Election Day, Melissa, a schoolteacher, also had the day off. The park was already overrun with harried-looking parents and adrenalin-pumped kids but when Melissa showed up, hair in signature ponytail and sporty backpack, she looked refreshed and relaxed.

Although Taryn wasn't much of a hugging person, she found herself almost immediately engulfed in an embrace that smelled like gardenias and Ivory soap. "I am so glad to see you, girl," Melissa beamed. "I was hoping you'd invite me up here."

"To be honest, I figured you'd done so many field trips here you would be sick of it," Taryn teased her.

"Yeah, well, this is different. I don't get to see a friend often and spend the day with her."

Taryn preened a little at the idea of someone referring to her as a "friend" and began leading Melissa through the gate. "We can grab lunch around noon, if that's okay. In the meantime I thought we'd start at the farm and then kind of work our way to the other end."

"Sure, lead on!"

Melissa's husband's family had owned the adjoining farm to the house where Taryn had last worked in Kentucky. Many years ago, one of his relatives had disappeared and that mystery haunted the town and family for generations. Not only had Taryn helped solve it, Melissa had been instrumental in putting the pieces together with her. They'd also shared a truly terrifying experience neither would ever forget. Now the two women chatted and laughed about the British royal family, new horror movie remakes of old films, and whether or not it was appropriate to wear pajama bottoms in public.

"I mean, really," Melissa ranted as they left the shop that featured weaving demonstrations. "It's not just that they wear the pajamas, they wear those old flannel ones that fray at the bottom when they drag the ground too much."

"My grandmother would throw a fit," Taryn agreed. "I understand being comfortable but at what point do you draw the line?"

"And you know those are probably the same people who get mad if you look at 'em cross-eyed," Melissa cackled.

Taryn was thoroughly enjoying herself, almost forgetting that there was a mystery at hand and that she'd been virtually attacked not once, but twice, by some kind of evil entity.

By the time they got to the other end of the park Taryn's legs were starting to throb and her lower back was killing her. She hated to complain but needed something to ease the pain. The embarrassment of admitting to Melissa that she was uncomfortable was just too great, however. Instead, she suggested they stop at the edge of one of the barns, near the cemetery, and take a break.

"I'm not as young as I used to be," she wheezed as she flopped to the ground, wincing as the hard surface brushed against her bones.

Melissa had noticed her discomfort but was too polite to mention it. "I hear that," she agreed. "So, give me the scoop. What's been going on?"

"Oh, you know, the regular. Camera sees ghosts, unsolved mystery, and I'm trying to figure it out before the job runs out," Taryn chortled. "Just another day in my non-career."

"'Non-career'," Melissa echoed. "What's that supposed to mean?"

"Nothing," Taryn said with a wave of her hand. "Just this guy here, working on a book. He doesn't believe this is really a viable job and that I make money at it. He's either complaining that they hired me or trying to figure out if I make actual money at it."

"Oh, screw him," Melissa said in disgust. "He's probably mad that he's not doing it."

They laughed together and there, in the sunlight, Taryn felt so normal that a feeling of contentment rose up in her stomach and actually threatened to linger. Was this what it was like to have a girlfriend? To hang out with a friend who made you laugh, cared about you? Taryn had never had a close friend; indeed, her only real friends had ever been Matt and Andrew.

A huge part of Taryn wanted to cling to Melissa, to desperately hold onto her and make her love Taryn so much that she'd never think about leaving the friendship. She'd so enjoyed writing emails back and forth over the past year, sending each other funny pictures on the internet, and now visiting again in person. She didn't want that to end. The few times in her life she'd been close to someone they'd left her, mostly for good. This fear of abandonment gave Taryn a sense of desperation that embarrassed her and caused her to feel an extraordinary amount of angst.

It was time for lunch, though, and they had reservations since the day was so busy.

"Can I take a look at Miss Dixie?" Melissa asked after they had risen from the ground.

"Sure," Taryn replied but when she reached down to pick her camera up, she lost her footing. Later she would admit it felt like something pushed her but for now all she felt was chaos of falling, tumbling down the small embankment and the final "thud" as she landed in the road, directly on her sore hip. She knew she was twisted like a pretzel and in pain she cried out, tears running down her face in betrayal.

"Oh my god, are you okay?" Melissa called out, springing into action. The mother in her came out in full force as she knelt next to Taryn and began pushing on her tenderly.

Taryn tried to nod but the pain was building now, a sharp stabbing that radiated from her hip down her leg and to her foot. Then, in defeat, she shook her head.

"I think you've dislocated it," Melissa stated with authority. "That can happen easily with your condition, right?"

Taryn groaned. "But sometimes we can get it back it..."

With an obscene amount of effort, Taryn attempted to stretch her leg out and twist her hip. The pain ripped through her then, like a knife, and she screamed in agony.

"I'm going to call for help," Melissa explained, whipping out her phone. Miss Dixie dangled from her arm; she'd picked it up when she took off after Taryn's slide.

She'd no more than dialed the numbers when the air changed, charged with electrical power that knocked both women back. Melissa fell to the ground now, Miss Dixie held protectively in front of her. In bewilderment she looked at Taryn for an answer but Taryn's gaze was transfixed on what was happening before her. As she continued to whimper in pain, the male figure appeared before her, kneeling at her feet. The look of sheer panic on his face, the terror, touched Taryn.

He's afraid for me, she thought. That's almost sweet.

But while he was looking at her, he didn't seem to be seeing her. Instead, he reached for Taryn's leg, his face white and scared. When his lips moved, raspy words shot out like burnt leather–a voice that hadn't been used for more than a century.

"You'll be alright," he murmured, but his voice shook. He was doing something to her, petting her? His hands worked furiously as he touched her hip, stroked her leg, fumbled at her knee, and then went back to her waist. She could feel nothing but warm air as his hands passed through her.

And then sadness overtook his fear. As his face contorted in despair he gazed down at his own hands, crossed over one another before him. "Oh heavenly father," he prayed. "Oh what did we do? What did we do?" He rocked back and forth, singing a sweet, sad song with lyrics Taryn had heard someplace before.

She reached out to touch him, to offer comfort through her own pain, and tried to speak. "Morgan?" she ventured tentatively. "Morgan?"

He looked up sharply, not at her but at something far beyond her. His face contorted in rage, explosive anger. Fire sparked his eyes and his hands clenched in steel.

With a mighty roar he opened his mouth and bellowed a thunderous cry. The crows on a nearby limb took a flight, their wings flapping furiously as they beat against the wind.

And just as before, he was gone.

"Oh my god, oh my god," Melissa chanted. "Oh my god."

"He tried to help me, though," Taryn cried. The pain was returning with a vengeance now that he was gone and her mind could go back to it. "Right?"

"Oh, Taryn," Melissa sobbed. Taryn was confused to see the sadness, rather than fright, on Melissa's face. She was holding Miss Dixie out to her, the LCD screen bright. "I thought I could take-after last time you know...a picture?"

Taryn reached out her hand and took the camera and focused on the image. It became immediately clear why Melissa was crying.

Taryn had been confused, understandably so. The man hadn't been taking care of her, he'd been taking care of someone else from long, long ago. Although moments before he'd knelt by Taryn and there had been nothing but empty air between them, in the picture Melissa captured in haste, his hands were full of a very real, and obviously lifeless, infant.

The local hospital was able to get her hip back to where it was

supposed to be and gave her a shot of morphine while she was there. Although it took up most of the day and Taryn was upset her afternoon with Melissa was ruined, she took solace in the fact that she didn't have to spend the night.

Melissa waited with her in the hospital and then drove her back to the park.

"I really thought I'd seen it all," Melissa mused as she sped through the quiet streets. "After what I saw and heard at the other house...but I believe this takes the cake."

"Yeah, well, it's a first for me, too," Taryn admitted with serenity. They'd given her a shot of morphine for the road so she was feeling pretty good about life in general at the moment. Maybe she'd start her own opiate garden at home. Though she doubted she could plant enough poppies on her apartment's balcony to bring in much of a crop.

"And I know it's inappropriate to bring this up but the ghost guy? He was kind of hot," Melissa blushed. "You know, in a dead kind of way."

Taryn had to agree with her there. He was hot. Extremely.

"Hey, did you talk to Matt?" she asked suddenly, remembering the texts he'd sent her while she was talking to the nurse.

"Yes and I did everything I could to keep him at home. But that boy is stuck on you and was chomping at the bit to come take care of you," Melissa warned her, glancing over at Taryn in the passenger seat.

Taryn grimaced, eyes half closed. Maybe she'd just take a little nap...

"Seriously. My husband and I have been together for more than six years and I don't think I've ever heard him that concerned."

Matt did worry about her; she knew that. And she worried about him. She loved him. But for a second the ghost-Morgan had looked at her with such passion in his eyes that she'd been transported to someplace else. The fact that he wasn't really seeing her was irrelevant. Was it imagination-cheating if the other person was dead?

"The girl he was seeing," Taryn began softly, feeling like she was being lifted up into the clouds, "her name was Evelyn. She's dead now."

Melissa smirked. "Yes, I figured that. I didn't think these people were one hundred fifty years old. Although I guess it's possible Shaker Town does have a fountain of youth nobody knows about."

Taryn laughed. "They must have been friends, maybe more. She had a baby. She was attacked by somebody. I don't know who. Or maybe the baby was Morgan's and that's why he was murdered."

"Morgan is the guy who was killed, right?" Melissa mused thoughtfully as she turned into the park. "Well maybe your Evelyn killed him."

"Why?" Taryn asked, genuinely perplexed.

"If they were lovers or he raped her or...I don't know," Melissa replied. "Lots of reasons to kill someone."

"But he loved her. You could see that."

"Love is an even stronger reason to kill someone," Melissa chuckled. "Just wait until you're married."

Taryn groaned to herself, resisting the urge to speak out about Andrew. They had been married in every sense but the legal one. And she'd never wanted to kill him. Well, almost never.

"I mean it," Melissa insisted. "Some mornings I wake up and look at my husband and think, I could kill him or I could make breakfast. Then I think about the effort of cleaning up the blood, the expense of the funeral, and how hard it is to find a babysitter these days. So I'll get up and put on the coffee."

Taryn laughed.

Melissa helped Taryn up the stairs and into bed. She even darted off to the vending machines and brought her back plenty of caffeine and snacks.

"You sure you don't want me to stay?" she asked worriedly, looking around Taryn's room to see if there was anything else she could do.

Taryn very much wanted her to stay; she didn't want to be alone. But she could never say that. "No, I'm fine. When these wear off I'll take one of my other ones. It will be hard to walk on for a day or two but it won't kill me."

She apologized again for ruining their afternoon and Melissa waved it off. "Oh, please. I have more excitement with you than I've ever had with anyone in my life. I mean, come on. Something wild happens every single time I see you. Seriously. And...it helps a little."

"What do you mean?" Taryn was propped up with a bunch of pillows behind her back, too many really but she didn't want to hurt Melissa's feelings by rearranging them. She'd worked very hard on making Taryn comfortable.

Melissa gently lowered herself to the side of Taryn's bed and let out a huge sigh. "I've never really been the religious type. You know, like everyone else around here I grew up going to church, going to Bible school, singing the right songs at the right time. That kind of stuff. But the actual believing part has always been a little hard for me. Sometimes I think the only reason I believe is because I am afraid it might all be true and I don't want to be left in the dust flames, as it may be."

Taryn nodded her head. Boy, *could* she understand.

"I've never seen anything amazing. Never looked at anything as being part of God's work or whatever. Someone might look at a sunset and say, 'Look what God painted' and I'd always look at it and think natural gases and stuff, you know?"

Taryn said she did.

"If someone said they saw a ghost then I'd listen to their stories about their dead grandparent or whatever. And it's not like I thought they were lying or anything, but a big part of me was skeptical. And then I met you. What I saw at that farm...it changed everything I'd ever believed in. It made me believe in what I'd always wanted to believe in."

Taryn was amazed. She'd never thought in a million years that the horror of Windwood Farm had made such an impact on Melissa. "Yeah, I get that I guess. It does make you start reevaluating what's going on around you. I was always a little skeptical myself."

"I know for a fact that there's something else out there, now, something bigger than me. I have no idea what it is but it changes things. I know that faith is believing but I am not built like that. I have to see to believe. And I saw."

178

A little light exercise was actually good for Taryn's leg and hip

so she tried doing a few laps around her room. The morphine wore off quickly, it always did, and then she was stuck with her normal pain. She made sure to rub her gel down her legs and take her vitamins and drink her tea (followed by her Coke because living without caffeine was just wrong).

By 8:00 pm she was ready to get out and get moving. Traveling down the stairs was difficult and she realized halfway down them that it was probably a bad idea to even try, but by that time she was almost there and didn't want to give up.

Since it was getting closer to summer the sun was staying out later now. The dusky sky was sleepy, the rooftops rosy in its light. Taryn didn't want to go far so she walked to a bench and sat down to enjoy the evening air. A slow breeze tickled the nape of her neck and lifted her hair. The park manager and Lydia had both come by to check on her and offer her food but she'd resisted. Her stomach was a little upset from the morphine still. The outside air, though, was straightening her and she was beginning to feel the pains that came with going too long without eating.

Matt had sent her half a dozen texts and called her twice. He wanted to come up. She wanted to see him, but she didn't want to be taken care of at the moment. She wanted to see him when she was feeling well and in control, not because she needed someone to come to her rescue. It happened a lot with Matt; she depended on him to fix things for her. It felt like less of a partnership sometimes than caretaker and she needed to change that. With Andrew they had been in everything together. With Matt one of them was always "in charge;" as kids it had been her with her brashness and boldness, as adults it seemed to be him with his organization and even temper.

She thought she'd pieced together the story of the murder, at least with the information she had. She thought it obvious that Evelyn was pregnant, probably by Morgan, and that the baby had died. Then someone had killed him and she'd left. The "someone" had to be the awful thing that kept attacking her, but she didn't know what it was yet. She didn't believe in demons, or that demons could attack people, but without a face she didn't know what else to call it. Evelyn, either before or after Morgan's death, had taken her brother and moved into town with family where they had, apparently, lived happily ever after.

She actually felt pretty good with herself for putting it together. She'd solved the big murder mystery of Shaker Town, although little of it had been through bonafide research. She'd have a hard time explaining to others how she'd reached her conclusions, of course.

A door slammed in the distance, a noise that sounded like it came from another realm. Taryn looked up and saw a figure hunched over, running. They wore an old-fashioned cloak that was tied around their neck so that she was unable to see if they were male or female. The figure ran from the site of the old house, a place that only had a small structure still standing, and darted off into the woods. Another employee? Maybe. Their movements had been graceful, though harried, and the cloak had billowed out behind them like Gothic wings, almost black.

Moments later Taryn heard a scream, a deep bellowing that sang of pain and anguish. It continued on, reverberating through her and echoing from the dark hole of the ice house. Nobody else seemed to hear or notice, despite the fact there were several other tourists milling about the grounds.

Curious, Taryn stood and hobbled painfully towards the small group of trees, making sure she didn't step in a hole or over a root–something that might cause her to trip and make things worse.

When she reached the edge, the last of the sun had dipped over the hills and the light was muted now, colorless. It was quiet; the moaning had stopped for the time being. Still, Taryn had walked all that way...

There wasn't much to see, just a small plaque and shards of stone sticking up out of the space in the ground. She strained to read the words on the plaque, taking in the history of the fairly advanced technology that had allowed the Shakers to store their food in fairly modern ways. So intent on the words, she was, that she didn't notice the thick dirty fog that was starting to curl around her feet and lick at her ankles. It soared up about her, lapping like a hungry wolf. By the time Taryn looked down and noticed it, the fog was nearly to her waist, the thickness of it disturbingly impenetrable. She couldn't see the ground below, or her lodgings back behind her. She was enclosed in a circle now, cut off from the rest of the world, although she could still hear the low rumblings of the other tourists who couldn't have been more than one hundred yards away.

Taryn kicked at the fog, tried to brush it off her, but it clung to her clothes like briars, digging into her with sticky thorns. The sound of anguish returned then, beginning as a low moan that was distinctly male and gradually increasing until it was the unmistakable sound of torture. Whoever was hurt was in an immense amount of pain, the noises gurgling in his throat like a wet bubble. She heard him choke, spit something, and then resume the awful sound of near begging for his suffering to end.

Taryn felt for him, she was human after all, and yearned to reach out and help. She could see nothing beyond her, however, and though the torment sounded like it was surrounding her and coming from all directions at once, she couldn't see a single source.

For a terrible moment Taryn thought she might be stuck there, forever trapped in that void. *This must be what hell is like,* she thought with panic. Not the everlasting fire and vicious heat of the stories but this blind, dirty, nothingness and terrible stench that choked and grabbed at you until you went insane.

In panic, she stretched out her arms, as much for balance from the fog that threatened to knock her over as to touch something that would serve as a reminder she was still alive. Her fingers grasped at thin air, the tips turning cold as ice. She thought of her mother, a woman who'd barely had the time to show her any interest, and silently cried for her. She saw Matt behind her eyes, his sweet dark face panicking and searching for her, knowing instinctively that she was in trouble.

"Matt, Matt!" she called frantically. "Please." It was one word but it broke something around her and the air began to part a little. The temperature rose just a few degrees so she focused on him again: his deep-set eyes, his soft black hair, his long elegant fingers...She remembered kissing him, the way her forehead fit against his in a perfect fit, his skinny legs poking out of his too-big khaki shorts. Then she remembered being kids with him, riding their bikes at top speed down the big hill in their housing development, squealing together as they charged off into their fantasy land they'd created, just the two of them. She could almost feel her hair flying out behind her, the rush of the wind against her face, the wheels turning and turning under her, bringing her faster and faster to a destination that would never be as exciting in real life as it was in her mind.

The fog parted with deftness now, leaving her exposed, standing in the field by the former ice house, her arms still outstretched. A family with two small children walked by and glared at her, like she might have been on drugs (well, they weren't entirely wrong) and ushered their children on. Nothing to see here, folks.

Taryn's breath erupted in a blast, the wind knocked out of her. She hadn't realized she'd been holding it. Her phone was ringing like crazy, Matt's ring tone. She couldn't count on her fingers to work to answer it. It would have to wait.

It was completely dark now; she didn't know how long she'd been standing there but it must have been a little while. As she began to hobble away, a rustle caught her ear and she turned back, probably against her better judgment. A long, thick, pale arm appeared in the shards of rock. It clawed out of them, the body it was attached to covered by something she couldn't see. The skin was thickly splattered with what she thought was tar at first and then saw it for the blood it was. The wet liquid gleamed in the moonlight like black ice. The hand scraped at the air, reaching for something it couldn't grasp.

Taryn didn't wait to see what would happen next. She'd had enough for the day.

CHAPTER 15

"Hey, how you holding up?" Dustin asked, worry

lining his face.

Taryn was still having trouble standing and in an effort to cause no further damage had set up a chair outside next to her easel. She could lower the easel and paint easily enough from her seated position, although she preferred to stand. Taryn's favorite way to paint was barefoot, digging her feet into the dirt and feeling the soft grass beneath them. It made her feel closer to the world around her, like she was more than just an observer.

She was making do with the chair, though, and had set up a small table with her drinks, iPod stand, and paints. It was almost like she had her own little living room right there in the middle of the park.

"I'm doing okay," Taryn replied, a little uncomfortable. Everyone had been so nice to her, stopping to see her and check on her. Eddie Jay had even dropped by with some banana nut bread his "wife" baked for her. (Park gossip said she wasn't his wife at all, but a woman he hung out with at a local bar who sometimes came in and cleaned for him.)

"Lydia said that if you needed anything just give us a call. With her at one end and me at the other we could meet in the middle and take care of anything you need," he said.

"I think I'll be okay," she smiled.

Like just about every place she worked, she was getting attached to Shaker Town. She hated to leave now, despite the ghosts. She even played around with the idea of applying for a full-time job, or volunteer as a docent. She could see herself living in one of the cute little houses in Burgin or Harrodsburg. Or even commuting in from Lexington. She liked Lexington. But the idea was totally unrealistic, unless she wanted to change careers.

Still...

Taryn had recently become aware of a woman nearby who went into old houses and businesses when they were about to be torn down or renovated and salvaged fixtures. She took doors, fireplace mantles, light fixtures, staircase banisters...Then she sold them at her store off the beaten path in downtown

Lexington. Taryn hoped to be visit it soon. How could you go wrong with a name like "Cowgirl's Attic?" She'd always felt like a cowgirl at heart. And besides, that sounded like her dream job. If she could only combine that with her painting, she'd be all set. Who knew, Lexington was a little artsy. Maybe she could open her own gallery...

But she was woolgathering, like she tended to do when she was working. It was easier to get lost in thought when her hands were busy and her mind free to wander.

In the end, she hadn't been able to hold Matt off. When Carol informed her that they were extending her contract another week, against Taryn's protests, Matt decided he'd been away long enough. He would be arriving at the airport the next morning and Taryn was both excited and nervous about seeing him. The park was hers at the moment: her mystery, her ghosts, her peace. When she and Matt were together, something else happened. They fed off one another in more ways than one and whatever sensitivities she had become stronger, if that was possible. Now what was going on would be partly his, too. It almost didn't seem fair.

The follow-up appointment with the orthopedist was in Lexington which meant Taryn had another long drive ahead of her. Since she couldn't take anything strong while driving, she'd cut herself off in advance, just to make sure there wasn't anything in her system that might impair her.

Maneuvering down Nicholasville road at 9:00 am wasn't the most pleasurable activity she'd ever done (all those lanes, all those cars, all those pedestrians who had death wishes) but it was kind of exciting. Once she'd parked at the large research hospital and was in the shuttle bus to the main building she finally took a sigh of relief.

Guest Services had tracked her down just before she left; she had a package. Rob's books had come through for her, finally, and she had them safely tucked inside her knapsack. She figured she'd have a lot of time for reading while she waited. These things always took forever. Just explaining her medical conditions alone took up half the visit.

There were three books in total: the promised-collection of ghost stories, what looked like a heavy book of text-heavy history stuff, and a loosely bound older book that, at quick glance, showed copies of journals and letters.

Once she got settled into the cold, antiseptic waiting room, she pulled them from her bag and began flipping through the pages. The first one was the book of Shaker ghost stories. They were fun reading, but mostly the "bump in the night" kinds of stories she was used to hearing. She saw her woman in white pop up a few times, along with stories of ghosts helping other people, taking strolls across the lawn, turning lights off and on, and singing. Typical ghost stories. Towards the end, however, there was one that made her sit up straight. It came from a contributor simply listed as "John" and was dated 1987.

"I was at the park for a wedding and it had just grown dark. It had been a long day and my girlfriend and I were fighting. I took a walk to cool off and found myself down at the pond. It was the only place I could find that was quiet and away from everyone else so I sat on the bench under one of the big trees. A few minutes later, I heard footsteps approaching. Thinking it was someone from the wedding, I turned around, ready to be annoyed. Couldn't I have even a few minutes to myself? It wasn't one of the guests, however. This was a man, wearing a long cloak and an old-fashioned hat pulled low over his eyes. Then I thought, you know, it was an interpreter. Maybe I wasn't supposed to be there. I was getting ready to apologize but he walked right past me. He didn't pay any attention to me and just went to the pond. He was carrying something in his hand but I couldn't see what it was. I watched him for a minute, you know, and he watched the water. I started to call out to him and see if everything was okay but then I noticed that something was dripping from his cloak. At first I thought it was water, that he'd cleaning something and got wet. But I've been a trauma nurse for a decade. That was blood. It ran off his cloak in streaks and dripped onto the ground. Before I could stand up and walk away, he disappeared."

The story jived with what she knew about the pond being haunted, as well as what she'd seen. It was amazing "John" had seen him so clearly. He must be a sensitive and not know it, Taryn thought.

It was in the last book, however, that she found what she needed: A journal entry written in 1866 had her stopping in her tracks and gasping aloud. Several patients seated around her looked at her with mixtures of annoyance and curiosity. She read it once, then twice, then again.

The beginning of the entry was innocent enough–talks of harvest and grain, of taking things to town to sell. It was written by a caretaker and who seemed to have his pulse on everything going on around him. Then there was this:

"Naturally, the elders are concerned with these recent events, especially when taken into consideration the tragedy that occurred in the ice house. There have been talks of handling such matters in a different, quieter, way in the future. Although the matter didn't reach outside to many its long arms touched all the Sisters and Brethren here in ways that many are still recovering from. The death, of course, was grisly enough but that the poor man was able to drag himself from his place of attack and seek help in the west dwelling was nothing short of a miracle. If only the miracle could have reached even farther. Despite the best medical care, the blood loss was too great, the lost limbs causing a shock none of us (especially him) could overcome."

It was true, then. Someone had been murdered and while not hacked to pieces, certainly suffered a loss of limb. Maybe more than one. And he'd almost certainly bled out right there in the foyer of the building she was staying in.

Taryn took this information in stride as she followed the nurse to her examination room. The elderly doctor poked and prodded at her, nodding at some things and raising his eyes at others. "Well," he boomed, "you're certainly flexible young lady!"

"Yes," she agreed, "I am." He currently had her "good" leg up over her head.

"And you say you have a lot of pain?"

"Not anymore than my usual pain," she answered.

"Well, what's that from?" he asked, flipping through her chart. "You got something else?"

Taryn cocked her head to the side and studied him. "It's from the EDS."

"Oh, I don't think so," he chuckled. "EDS doesn't cause pain. Just makes you flexible."

Taryn resisted the urge to give him a lecture. Instead, she bit her tongue and smiled. "That's not what the menagerie of other specialists I see say."

"And where did you get this alleged diagnosis," he asked, making her face turn red.

"By one of the best geneticists in the world," she answered. "I was diagnosed both clinically and through gene testing."

"Well, you may or may not have it," he said, rubbing his hand over her arm. "You're hands are certainly smooth, though.

I guess it means you don't wash dishes." No, nitwit, she wanted to scream. It's one of the biggest hallmarks of EDS and one of the first things they look for—remarkably smooth and soft skin.

"That must be what it means," she said sarcastically.

"Have you heard of the Beighton Scale?" he asked, asking her to stand.

"Um, yes. I score a 9/9 on it." The Beighton score took flexibility into account and was a clinical way of diagnosing hypermobility syndrome.

Then, to her shock, he started having her do her "tricks" to test it for himself. By the time he asked her to bend over and touch her toes, she was furious. "Look," she said at last. "I am not here to get a new diagnosis or for you to re-diagnose something I've already been diagnosed with. I am just here for a follow-up for my dislocation."

His eyes hardened now and he took a step back. "You think you know more than me?"

"Yes," she nodded, "I do. I see the top specialists in the country for this, keep current on all the latest research, and have literally tried every over-the-counter pill, supplement, gel, cream, and prescription that's offered. I can tell you anything you want to know about EDS, from start to finish, and then some. Because I live with it, and I like to be informed."

He listened to this with raised eyebrows, frowning. "Well, I am going to give you a steroid injection in your hip today and then send you to physical therapy for a month. Some stretching exercises should fix some things."

When he walked out of the room Taryn waited for a minute and then gathered her stuff and left as well, not waiting for him to return. Stretching exercises were the last thing she needed; her body's problem was that it was too stretchy. Stretching more could cause serious risks. And she'd already had an injection at the hospital. Another one could damage her connective tissue even more; people like her had to be careful with those.

For now, she'd just limp back to her car and drive back to her lodgings. You know, the place where a legless man had crawled into after being hacked by a crazy person and bled out at the bottom of the stairs? She'd rather be there than another minute in the examination room.

"Did you hear what happened at the park last night?" Julie

asked. Taryn was eating lunch with Julie, Dustin, and Ellen. They'd all come to her and found her in her room and were now camping out on her floor, food spread about them. She was touched; it felt a little bit like a party.

At first Taryn thought she was referring to the horrible thing that happened at the site of the old ice house but then she realized Julie couldn't possibly know about that. "What happened?"

"You know that building they're restoring at the edge of the park? One of the shops...I can't remember which one," Julie admitted.

"I know what you're talking about," Taryn replied. "Everything okay?"

Julie leaned forward, her eyes big. "Someone broke into it and stole stuff. Like the copper but also some tools. Stupid for the workers to leave them in there. Everyone is super pissed. First me, then Andy, and now the park."

"I don't know. Andy probably deserved it. That dude wears me out," Dustin shuddered and popped a purple grape into his mouth.

"Geeze," Taryn said. "Why would someone steal from Shaker Town?"

Dustin shook his head then shrugged. "Money I guess," he answered philosophically. "I guess when you think you need it you'll do just about anything."

"Then why not keep a job," Julie snapped, crinkling her nose in disgust. "The rest of us have one."

Lydia frowned. "We have jobs and we're still poor. You know our house is going through foreclosure?"

Taryn did not know but felt instant sympathy for them. They held themselves together so well. She often saw Dustin and Lydia walking through the park together, holding hands and laughing after work. Sometimes, when they thought nobody was looking, he'd sneak over from the farm and give her a very unchaste kiss behind the trees or in the shadow of the meeting house door.

"What happened?" Taryn asked and then blushed. "I mean, if you don't mind me asking. I know it's none of my business."

Lydia looked down at her dress and picked an invisible piece of lint off it. "A few years ago we had a...health problem," she said softly.

Taryn nodded. "I understand. I have some health issues too, a rare connective tissue disorder. My insurance isn't great and every time I check the mail I find I owe more money from some test, lab, or specialist visit."

Dustin signaled his sympathy and then reached for Lydia's hand. "We were pregnant and *didn't* have insurance. We made it to the eight month and then there were some issues. Lydia developed preeclampsia and had a complete placental abruption. She delivered early and he was born sleeping."

Taryn looked at the couple in horror, unable to speak. Julie looked stunned as well; it was clear she did not know this information about them.

"Oh my God," Taryn murmured, wanting to reach over and hug them both but not really knowing where her boundaries were. "I am soooo sorry. And even sorrier I compared my stupid health issues with yours."

"It's okay," Lydia smiled with her mouth but the rest of her face was stone cold. "It's been four years. We had a lot of bills after that, though. The hospital bills, after care bills, burial bills...not to mention what we'd already spent on Carter."

"We got pregnant again after that but Lydia's uterus ruptured," Dustin explained, "and it had to be removed. So no more kids for us."

"And that meant *more* bills," Lydia added bitterly.

"But we're okay. We *will* pay them," Dustin assured her. "It meant we got behind in our house payments, though. We're trying to pull it out but it's hard. I freelance in IT and she makes jewelry on the side and sells them at craft fairs but we feel like we're constantly working to dig ourselves out."

Taryn could understand how that felt. It seemed like the more money she earned the higher her bills got. She couldn't get ahead. She was grateful, though, that she hadn't asked either one of them about the infants haunting the pond. That would've been terrible, although she hadn't known their history.

"Anyway, we didn't mean to bring the party down," Lydia put in. "It's always a downer."

"It's just so sad," Julie all but wailed, her youthful sympathy both touching and over the top. "To plan for something like that and then it all just fall apart."

"Yeah, well, the idea was not something we talked about at first," Dustin admitted. "We hadn't been married long and kids wasn't even on the table."

"I was terrified when I first found out I was pregnant," Lydia agreed, casting a glance over at him. "I cried and cried. He tried to take me out to celebrate and all I could do was bawl. I was a mess. I just saw our lives ending, my youth over, being tied to someone you were responsible for. It all felt like too much."

"And then we picked up this baby book and read about pregnancy and went to the first doctor's visit," Dustin interjected.

"It changed then. It was a slow build up, but we got excited. So, yeah, it was like having the rug pulled out from under you. I wouldn't wish it on anyone."

After Dustin and Lydia left, Julie helped Taryn straighten up a little. Taryn didn't expect maid service while she was there, and had asked not to receive it, so they just sent her new towels and sheets every few days. Julie helped her stack them in the bathroom and change her bedding. While she worked, she chatted away.

I had zero idea about Dustin and Lydia," she said, expertly slipping the feather pillow into the tight case. "Man, that was awful."

"Yeah," Taryn agreed. "That was pretty bad. Do you ever think about having kids?"

Julie stopped, the pillow dangling in the air. "I do sometimes. I love the idea of kids, you know? But I don't have a boyfriend right now so it's definitely not in the cards at the moment unless I pick someone up from a biker bar."

Taryn laughed and cleared off the trash on her desk. "Well, there's always that."

"And then there's the pain," Julie continued. "Maybe if they put me to sleep first. What about you?"

Taryn thought of Matt, of what kind of parent he would be. Would he be strict? Anal retentive? Would he play with the kids or be more of a big kid himself? Would he be able to handle their messiness? It was a lot to consider.

She had no problem imagining Andrew as a father. They'd talked about kids a lot. But he'd had a nephew, too, so she'd seen him in action. It wasn't fair, of course, to compare the two. She knew that and silently scolded herself.

"I think about it sometimes, but just kind of in a theoretical sense. You know, I wonder what a child of mine would look like. Wonder what they'd act like. But I have a hard time seeing myself as a mother," she admitted. "I don't know that I have the motherly instinct. I'm always by myself, I get annoyed when my time has to belong to someone else. I'm stubborn and bossy," Taryn laughed.

"Yeah, well, we're all a little like that," Julie pointed out. "It's human nature, after all."

Taryn thought she had a point. Maybe she wasn't as unique in these thoughts as she figured she was.

"Hey, so tell me about your boyfriend," Julie pleaded, bouncing on the freshly-made bed and making herself at home.

"Don't you have work to do?" Taryn teased her.

"Nope. Just came to pick up my check. I'm off today. So what's he like?"

Taryn settled in beside her and leaned back on the pillow. "Well, I've known him since I was a kid. And I mean a little kid. He was a weird child and so was I. We didn't have many friends at that age, just each other. Kind of ran in a posse of other kids but they didn't have much to do with us, truth be told. We clung to each other. It lasted through middle school, high school, college..."

"Sounds romantic," Julie gushed. "Like your childhood sweetheart. So have you always been together?"

"No," Taryn said. "We actually only just started dating recently. I was in a long-term relationship after college and was going to marry him. His name was Andrew."

Even now, saying his name filled her with both thrill and sadness.

"Wow, what happened? Did you leave him at the altar?" Julie pressed, eyes shining.

"No, he died in a car crash. We lived together, worked together, spent almost every minute together. And then he was just gone. It took me a long time to adjust and during that time Matt and I had a falling out. I didn't exactly handle Andrew's death very well."

"Yeah, well, who would?" Lydia argued. "There is no real 'right way' or 'wrong way' to handle someone's death. I lost my best friend from high school from a heroin overdose. He was nineteen. He was living alone at the time and they didn't find him until he'd been dead for almost twenty-four hours. It was terrible. That was a few years ago and I am still struggling with it."

"I'm sorry," Taryn said simply. Sometimes life was just too sad to bear. It broke your heart over and over and over again.

S omething was calling Taryn outside. It wasn't a voice or even

a sound at all. It was a tugging sensation, a pull towards something she didn't understand. She'd just washed the paint off her hands and was laying her brushes out to dry on a towel spread out on her bureau when she felt it. There was an urgency, a prodding, she couldn't ignore.

She didn't think about what it might mean for her or how silly it sounded; she simply slid on her sandals, grabbed her room key, and slung Miss Dixie around her neck. Despite the throbbing that still persisted in her hip, she was downstairs in a matter of minutes.

Almost as if she were swimming through molasses, Taryn made her way down the sidewalk, to the thoroughfare. She didn't know where she was going. It was evening now and the last bell had rung for the day. The doors were all closed and locked, except for the ones that housed accommodations, and small electric candles burned brightly from many of the windows. A friendly chatter could be heard from those who waited outside the Trustee's Office, ready to go inside and eat. The remainder of the doors slammed to as employees put things up for the night, a flurry of car engines started and the roar of vehicle departures rumbled in the distance. Somewhere a lonely goat cried "Maaa! Maaa!"

Taryn ignored all of this.

She felt excitement, a rush of good things to come. Her heart felt light, her stomach was nearly in her mouth from jittery nervousness, and her steps were lighter than normal. The more she walked, the less pain she felt. The feeling in her hips and legs, usually a distraction, slowly melted away until it ceased altogether. With the lack of pain she was able to pick up her pace and hurry. Miss Dixie bounced against her chest, and she wasn't a lightweight candle, but Taryn was able to ignore the "thumping" and smacking against her breastbone.

A smile spread across her face from ear to ear. Why, she was almost a young girl again, still in high school. Back when she looked forward to getting up every morning, getting dressed, and racing off to school because she had a crush on Joey Moody and she couldn't wait to see him. Oh, the thrill of flying down the hall to her locker and unloading her books, slipping into the dingy bathroom to reapply her lipstick, and then scurry to her homeroom where he'd be waiting. To catch that first glimpse of him, sitting in the back and goofing off with his friends, his dark jeans with the tear in the left knee and his wavy mullet...that had been pure bliss. (Of course he'd never noticed Taryn and she'd never actually spoken to him, except once in English when they had to read lines from a play out loud together in front of the class.) But those passionate teenage hormones had driven her, propelled her forward every single day.

She'd never felt like that since. Until now.

If she didn't get there soon it would be too dark to take pictures. She looked at the diminishing light and down at her camera. Miss Dixie's flash wasn't what it used to be; well, they were both getting older. Her bulb wasn't always the brightest anymore either.

Soon, Taryn arrived at her destination. She found herself standing where she'd only been just an hour before–outside the old schoolhouse. It looked spooky at night, one of the few buildings at the park that wasn't illuminated by the quaint street lamps or adorned with the vintage-inspired candles. Now it was just a dark shadow, black against the deep blue sky. The moon was full, giving Taryn more light than usual, but slivers of white clouds hung low around it, threatening to cover its glow.

The excitement continued to build, however, and Taryn felt downright giddy. She was literally shaking as she turned Miss Dixie on and pointed her at the structure. The flash was a startling contrast in the darkness, the small bulb light a spotlight that blinded everything in its path. Black dots swam in front of Taryn's eyes when she pulled away and the flashes of light continued to dance in the night in front of her, despite the fact Miss Dixie was finished with her part.

She only needed to take one picture. She knew that. The building before her was in shambles, the way it had been all along; the building in her photograph was perfectly restored with a sweet little white picket fence running around it. A light was on inside. Taryn's eyes rolled back in her head then, a dizziness overtaking her that made her incredibly nauseous. The lights continued to flash in front of her, what she thought were delayed tricks of the light from her camera. But then the warmth overtook her, a sedating feeling, like she'd had Benadryl and was on the cusp of falling asleep. When she looked up this time, the building before her smiled, a candle in the window, the gate wide open and welcoming.

CHAPTER 16

*T*he room was hushed when she entered, the little

desks lined up in neat rows, all facing the front of a room where a larger desk and chair stood gleaming. It was quiet and empty. These students were dismissed a very long time ago. Small touches had been used to give it a homey appearance while maintaining the Shaker ideals: a wildflower arrangement was on the teacher's desk, colorful rag rugs distributed around the floor, someone had drawn a rainbow on the chalkboard. There weren't any pictures on the walls; Shakers had not only shunned ornaments for simplicity reasons but because they gathered dust and made cleaning harder.

Although Taryn could see all of these things, they weren't quite solid. There was an otherworldly look to them, like she was gazing at the scene through goggles that had just been underwater. She yearned to reach out, run her fingers over the little chairs and down the freshly-painted walls, but was afraid. She didn't even want to breathe, so afraid she was of making it all vanish as quickly as it had appeared.

Her trembling fingers ached to turn Miss Dixie on, to try and capture everything her eyes refused to believe. She'd been given an incredible gift, she knew this a long time ago, but this went far beyond anything she'd ever imagined. Had she stumbled back in time? Was she dreaming? Was she dead? Had she accidentally doubled a dose of her pain meds and this was the end? Or was it all just an illusion Miss Dixie was helping bring to life for her?

She didn't care. She just wanted to enjoy it.

The situation was an odd one, to say the least, but fear was the last thing Taryn felt. The adrenaline rush was just too great.

She took a tentative step forward, testing the floor underneath her. It felt solid and real. Another test step put her closer to the middle of the floor and now she spun in circles, looking at everything in awe. Oh, if only she'd lived back then, she sighed. It all looked so much simpler, so beautiful. She ached to be a part of it all.

The door opened then and Taryn startled, panicked that her vision was going to waver and send her sprawling back into the modern night.

The woman walked through the door, however, and Taryn gasped as Evelyn moved right through her and went to the head of the class. She seemed not to notice Taryn and as she slid through her body, she moved as easily as if she were walking through steam or fog.

Evelyn's soft dark hair was piled on her head in a neat and tidy bun, the Shaker-style cap pinned firmly atop it. Her dress was long-sleeved with an apron over it. It was buttoned to the top of her neck, proper-like, but Taryn smiled a little when she took a quick look around the room and then loosened the top two. This revealed pale, creamy-smooth skin that was obvious even through the haze that Taryn watched her in.

She had a soft look about her, a beautiful girlishness that didn't come through in the stern, period photo she'd seen of her, or of the more recent one taken at the turn of the century when she'd been much older. This Evelyn was light on her feet, almost graceful, but Taryn knew this from having watched her in the meadow before. Up close, though, she had slender hands that moved as lightly as feathers as they stacked up leather-bound books, and tiny feet that looked no bigger than a child's. In fact,

Evelyn herself couldn't have been more than five feet tall, and that might have been pushing it. She was a small, delicate woman and seeing her in this manner, knowing what she knew about her fate, made Taryn ache to protect her.

Evelyn glanced up once, and then again, watching the back of the room. Although her eyes landed on Taryn each time they didn't see her. They were seeing something there from a long, long time ago.

Another noise filtered through the scene (it was the only way Taryn could think of it) and made her turn to the window. The mood in the room immediately changed. When Evelyn looked at the window as well and saw the form of the tall, curly-haired young man standing in the opening, an electric smile on his face and a hopeful look in his eye, Taryn felt like the room was going up in flames. How could anyone have missed the look that passed between them? The love, the bond, the kinship? There was a closeness between them conveyed in that one simple glance that Taryn knew wouldn't have been missed by anyone around them.

And oh, she was burning. The flames of jealousy cut through Taryn and stung her. There was a passion in the room now that Taryn couldn't remember having ever felt. It wasn't the strong bond of almost supernatural friendship she felt with Matt or the loyalty and comfort she'd had with Andrew, but a burning desire of love and devotion that somehow managed to cut through time and death. Taryn yearned to feel the same, felt her insides turning over.

Neither figures said a word, but they didn't need to. He bowed once, tipped his hat to her, and then moved away as quickly as he'd appeared. Evelyn turned back to her desk, a light fading from her eyes. She frowned then and sighed. That sound cut deep into Taryn and she felt for the young woman. Morgan's appearance had been the highlight of the day for her and Taryn suspected she'd probably looked forward to those visits and brief appearances as much as she'd looked forward to entering that long-ago classroom of her own, her eyes fixated on Joey Moody.

When the air changed again, the feel of the space did as well. Now it was charged with something hateful and powerful, as hard and burning as the jealousy she was feeling. Taryn knew that force well and knew what was about to happen. She could feel it moving through the back of the room, towards her and onto Evelyn. Evelyn looked up, panic flitting across her face. She tried to cover it with a smile but the smile was forced, panicked. The coldness and anger grew and threatened to choke Taryn again. Although she knew it would be the end of the gift she'd been given, she couldn't stand to watch the young woman suffer. It took every drop of energy and power she could possibly muster but at the top of her lungs she yelled, "Evelyn, RUN!"

And, for a split second, right before she was violently thrust back into the twenty-first century, she saw Evelyn's eyes meet hers and the two women held on to the other's gaze.

There wasn't enough alcohol in the world for what Taryn had

just experienced. In many ways, it was far more unsettling than some of the "scary" things that had happened to her in the past. She'd literally seen the past come alive, had watched Morgan and Evelyn in action. They were no longer one-dimensional figures in old, blurry photographs or names carelessly passed around–they were living, breathing people with passion and heat.

Taryn was still shaking as she climbed the stairs to go up to her room. She fumbled with her key and took three tries to get it in the lock. Once she was inside, she collapsed against the door and slid down to the floor.

Evelyn, or maybe it was Morgan, had wanted her to see that. She had no doubt in her mind that one of them had led her there, intent on her seeing the past and witnessing them in action. Maybe they'd wanted to show her that there was love between them, that neither could've possibly hurt the other.

And Taryn couldn't possibly forget the look in Morgan's eyes as he'd looked at Evelyn. There had been such tenderness, such joy, like just being in her presence had given him life. Taryn didn't think anyone had ever looked at her like that. Andrew had looked at her with love, with respect, and with admiration at times. Matt looked at her with a little bit of awe and reverence. She was, after all, the girl who'd scared off the bullies, protected him, and treated him like a real person. (The way he'd treated her.)

But now she found herself jealous of the ghosts. What they had was something else. And it wasn't fair. They were dead. Why did they still need it?

The jealousy formed in her stomach, a hard emotion she didn't recognize. It filled her with a coldness that ate at her and gnawed at her insides. It was an awful feeling and angered her. As though in agreement, a picture of a Shaker woman at a loom fell off her wall, the glass shattering on the floor into a million pieces. The curtains swirled and billowed out, like before, and as Taryn quickly rose to her feet, her closet door slammed to with a bang. Her hand crept behind her and found the knob. It was ice red hot under her touch and her delicate skin instantly blistered and burned. "Dammit!" she hollered, clutching it to her stomach and holding it there with her other one.

She was feeding it, whatever "it" was, and she knew it. As images of Morgan and Evelyn flashed through her mind and the jealousy grew, the dormant power in the room had festered. It had been waiting for her all along, just waiting for that moment when she provided it with enough ammunition to set it free.

And yet she couldn't stop herself. Horrible thoughts flew through her mind, thoughts about leaving Matt, of going far, far away and starting over on her own. Thoughts of being glad that Evelyn had been attacked, had given birth to a child who hadn't lived, that Morgan had been murdered...The more these thoughts gathered in her mind, the more ferocious the activity in her room became. Her makeup scattered off the sink in her bathroom, tubes of lipstick and fingernail polish flying onto the tile floor. Her paintbrushes, drying on the bureau, were tossed into the air one-by-one and dropped to the ground like little toy soldiers marching off into battle. The bed banged against the wall, the headboard loosening from the frame with each movement.

Taryn had zero control over any of this. She couldn't turn her mind off, she couldn't turn the activity off.

Painfully, she raised her still-throbbing hands to her eyes and covered them. "Stop," she sobbed. "Stop. I didn't mean it, I didn't mean it."

A low guttural noise filtered up beside her, slipping through the floorboards. Menacing and threatening, it growled near her feet, lapped at her waist, and pulled harshly at her hair much like the dirty fog by the ice house had. "No, just go away," she cried. She turned her thoughts to Matt, then, trying to forget what she'd been thinking just moments before. His eyes, his face, his hands...but the growling continued and now the pillows were flying off her bed, flying across the room and smashing into the wardrobe.

Panicked, her mind raced as she sought to find something to focus on. Her parents, her Aunt Sarah, Andrew...the names and faces flew before her eyes and with each one the cry grew louder, mocking her. She could feel its bites on her legs, on her lower back, on her thighs. And then, on her burning hand, she felt something hard, something she'd forgotten about. It was the ring that had belonged to her grandmother.

"Oh," she sobbed. "Oh!" Clutching the ring in her sore fingers she let it press into the burn, searing the blisters and cutting her flesh. Her grandmother's face appeared before her eyes, her sad smile and careworn face encouraging Taryn to keep trying, to keep moving.

When the last blister popped, the fluid spilling out over the old stone and faded gold band, the noise in her room stopped. One lonely paintbrush rolled off the bureau and fell with a "plop" to the floor and then rolled across the floor. It finally came to a stop by her foot, the red of the paint the color of the blood that spilled from her fingers and stained the ring she still clutched.

CHAPTER 17

*T*o Taryn's disappointment, Matt didn't seem to

appreciate Shaker Town nearly as much as she'd expected him to. She didn't count on him having her exact same interests, but sometimes they felt so far apart on the spectrum that she worried they wouldn't have enough to sustain them in old age, if it got that far. At the moment, their bond seemed to be rooted in a shared childhood and the ability to read one another's minds. She supposed other relationships had been built on less, but it felt like a slippery slope.

He ignored most of the quick tour she gave him on the way to her room, although he did express interest in her work and complimented her on that, and the only thing he cared about in her room was throwing her on the mattress, being careful of her hip, to "test it." But she supposed that was probably a guy thing.

"How was the flight up?" she asked. He'd already started unpacking his clothing, hanging his bathrobe on the hook behind the door, lining his toiletries out on the sink. In comparison to her things, his things were military-neat.

"It was okay. I had that layover in Charlotte and it lasted nearly three hours. I could've driven here in that time," he grumbled. "But I met a man who was reading Terry Pratchett in the rocking chair next to me and we talked about that for over an hour. It passed the time."

"Restaurant is busy today so I made us dinner reservations at 8:00 pm. They're doing barbecue tonight and it's very good. They've lit up the big grill thingie outside. It's why that side of the park smells like meat."

Matt's eyes lit up at this. There were few things he enjoyed talking about more than food. "That sounds very good. The last barbecue I had was at one of those chain places and it might as well have been shredded hot-dogs with ketchup."

"Well, you'll like this."

"By the way, I checked out that store you were talking about. That salvage place? On my GPS it looks like a fairly straight shot from here to there. If you want to go to Lexington tomorrow or something we could check it out."

She wanted to tell him that Lexington might have been a "straight shot" as far as the crow flew but navigating the roads, and then the traffic in some of the heavy areas of town, was anything *but* convenient. Still, it was sweet he was trying to think of her.

"I think that sounds good," she declared.

Taryn took him to some of her favorite places in the park and as the day wore on her mood elevated.

The whole time she'd been waiting for Matt to drive up in his rental car she'd been giddy, restless. She missed him tremendously and had visions of throwing herself at him, wrapping her legs around his waist, planting a long and passionate kiss on him. Sitting under the maple tree at the pond she'd daydreamed about the two of them barely able to make it back to her room, pawing one another shamelessly until they'd fallen through her door in a passionate heap.

Reality was a bit of a disappointment.

Rather than attacking each other in a fever the distance and time seem to have made them timid and shy with each other. The man she'd had a quickie with on the front seat of his car because they couldn't wait to get inside his house after a movie one night now stood and looked at her with nervousness, not knowing whether to kiss her or shake her hand. The dirty emails they'd shared over the past month or so seemed to have been written by other people.

It got better, however, the longer he was there. They'd worked up to holding hands as they walked, and after not touching for a long time even that felt erotic.

Although she'd become friendly with some of the employees, and even formed friendships with a few, having someone with her who was expressly interested in her was different. It gave her added confidence and made her feel more daring. Alone, she often walked quietly, not making eye contact, lost in her own head. With Matt, she chattered incessantly, stopping to point things out, and waved at people she'd come to know. They all looked at Matt expectantly, curiosity burning their faces. She'd only mentioned him to a few people, although a simple Google search would have connected him with her through some of the paranormal blogs, and they were probably wondering where he'd come from.

"I think I'm going to start telling people you were a tourist I picked up on the side of the road and had my way with," she teased him after a brief conversation with Eddie Jay.

"I'll go along with it," he shrugged, slipping his arm around her shoulder. "You want me to pretend to be a biker?"

Taryn pulled back and studied his pressed khaki slacks, golf T-shirt, and loafers. "Dear, I think they'd buy me as a biker before you. Unless you mean mountain biker."

When they got to the school Matt stopped and studied it. "Doesn't look like much from the outside, does it?"

Taryn shook her head. "No, not yet. But it will. They're very good at fixing these things up."

"What do you think caused the doorway opening?" Matt asked her as he walked up to the old window and ran his finger along the cracked wooden frame.

Taryn looked down at her feet. Her bright blue toenail polish was chipped. She'd forgotten that. She should've made more of an effort for Matt since she hadn't seen him in weeks. Her hair was still damp from the shower, too, not styled at all. In her mind she looked beautiful and becoming and in her "natural" state. In reality, without makeup, her hair styled, and her fingernails groomed she looked like she'd just walked out of a women's prison.

"I've been thinking about it," she admitted, "and now I can't help but wonder if I might have just been dreaming."

"Why would you say that?" Matt asked with interest. "You said you felt the floor under you, heard the noises, could see detail in their faces."

"I was also on some heavy drugs," she pointed out. "I had morphine in my system. I've looked at a ton of pictures, studied this building for weeks, and learned a lot about the Shaker schools. And, as you know, I have a very vivid imagination and create story lines in my head when I paint. This could've been the result of all those things mixing together in my head."

Matt didn't answer as they left the site and strolled to the pond. Taryn led him to the bench under the Maple tree and they sat together, hands touching, while they watched the water. There were children down there, throwing scraps of bread to the ducks. The ducks were skittish, wading off from the kids as quickly as they could, and a toddler charged after them, shrieking in a high-pitched babble that wasn't composed of real words.

Taryn thought Matt had forgotten about her comment back at the schoolhouse but, in typical Matt-style, he had just been thinking about it and trying to choose his words wisely. It often took Matt a while to process things. It's what made him a good scientist.

"Why would you talk yourself out of what happened?" he asked quietly. One of his fingers ran gently over her grandmother's ring, turning it around and around on her small finger. The blisters on her hand were gone; there was no sign she'd been in a struggle.

"I don't know," she shrugged petulantly, like a child. "Because it sounds too fantastical maybe?"

The truth was, she couldn't believe it had really happened, not in the clear light of day. It made her sound crazy, like maybe she needed mental help, and it scared her. What if she was going crazy, that it had all just been part of her medical condition? And, worse, what if it never happened again?

"You're afraid of believing it because you want it to happen again, aren't you?" Matt pressed. Still reading her mind.

Taryn nodded miserably.

"You were afraid of that with Miss Dixie, too," he pointed out. "And it continues to happen."

"This is different. This is like time travel. That's just weird. I mean, if you think about it, have you ever noticed that nobody ever talks about time travel? I mean, you see articles in the National Enquirer all the time about people who have seen ghosts, met aliens, and visited Satan. But where are the time travelers?"

"You mean the ones calling the paper and going, 'I just went back in time and you won't believe who killed Kennedy'– those people?" Matt smiled.

"Yes! It can't be real."

"As opposed to the people who were abducted by aliens and experimented on?"

"Hey, aliens could be real. It's an awfully big space out there."

"Taryn, did you ever think that maybe the lack of stories is the very thing that gives it some credibility? Maybe people don't remember when they travel back. Kind of the time paradox? And, did you ever stop to think that you weren't exactly traveling back in time but went inside Miss Dixie and was seeing her world?"

Taryn's eyes grew big and her mouth dropped open a little. No, she had not considered either one of those. "OH my God, that's why it was so hazy," she blurted out. "I went inside my own damn camera."

"I think so."

She aimlessly kicked at a small twig under her feet and sighed. "Yeah, like that's not any less weird."

"Miss Dixie has shown you things that need to make sense. You're not putting this together like you want to. This time she tried something else. Think about the things she must see and doesn't show you," he added.

The possibilities were endless and as Taryn gazed down at her camera she felt overwhelmed. The two of them worked together, her and her camera, and she didn't believe one really had much power without the other. But Miss Dixie seemed to have an unreasonable amount of supernatural ability for an electronic made in Southeast Asia.

"So Andy's a little bit of a weenie, huh?" Taryn laughed as they

walked back to her room in the darkness. The moon hung low in the sky, partially shielded by the clouds, and the lanterns glowed warmly around them. They were the only people out and if Taryn closed her eyes just for a moment she could pretend they'd stepped back in time again, two Shakers sneaking around in the night.

Then a park vehicle drove towards them, headlights bright and radio blaring Eminem, and that fantasy flew out the window.

"He's okay," Matt replied, always the diplomat. He didn't like to talk about people unless it was for a very good reason.

"I think he liked you, though," Taryn conceded. "He's been very rude to me."

They'd been seated with Andy at dinner, since they had reservations and he did not. Julie had caught her eye and sent her a sympathetic smile when she saw Andy pulling up a chair. The hostess, who didn't know Taryn well, clearly didn't realize the evening was the first she'd spent with Matt in a long time. Andy, in his booming "look-at-me" way, had chattered on and on, poking and prodding at Matt until he knew what his job title was, his annual income, and how much he'd paid for his house. Taryn was mortified but Matt took it in stride. By the end of the night, after Julie had sent several glasses of wine her way, Taryn had mellowed out a bit.

"The scientists I work with aren't always the most social creatures," he smiled, linking his arm through hers. "Myself excluded, of course. I'm a veritable extrovert compared to some of them. I'm used to putting up with some odd behavior."

It was a joke, of course. Matt was even more private than she was. His idea of a big night was making homemade ice cream and zoning out to a marathon of Star Trek episodes.

"Do you think you might be a little jealous of Andy?"

Taryn stopped in her tracks and looked at him in surprise. "What do you mean? I think he's jealous of me!"

Matt smiled a secret grin and looked down at her. "Andy's book will be in all the local bookstores. He'll do a book tour, get to travel. Sure it will be around the state but a few people will be very impressed. He'll make some money, get some speaking engagements. But your paintings..."

"Yeah, I know, Taryn grumbled. She unlinked her arm and stuffed her hands in the pocket of her cardigan. "Nobody ever looks at my name or knows who I am. Although I do get asked to do speaking engagements. Most of them are for paranormal research groups, of course..."

"Which you could do if you wanted. But that's not the point. You might make the money and have the freedom but Andy's work will garner him a lot of respect. And you wrote about the Shakers, too, for your dissertation. So maybe you both have a little bit of professional jealousy."

Taryn was appalled to realize he was probably right. "Well. Dammit."

It made her think, though, all the way back to her room. She did get invited to speak at paranormal conferences, to set up a vendor's table at conventions, and do Podcasts. She'd turned them all down, so far, but it didn't mean the ghost blogs and ezines hadn't picked up on her. Whether she did the interviews or not didn't stop them from writing about her. Maybe she should give in and realize that the paranormal thing was as much of a calling as the painting. Something else tugged at her in Matt's words, though. She approached it now with caution.

"Matt?"

"Yeah?" He was getting ready for bed, pulling down the blankets and fluffing the pillows. He'd already changed into his pajamas and brushed his teeth.

"Do you think I could write a book?"

"About your experiences? Or about the Shakers?"

"Neither," Taryn shook her head. "I was thinking more along the lines of a photography book. I take a lot of pictures. Maybe I could write one and include some of them? Not the ghost ones, those are too private, but maybe the ones with my old houses?"

Matt smiled and patted the spot beside him. Taryn bounced into bed and cuddled up next to him. "I think that's a grand idea," he announced, stroking her hair. "And I think you can do anything you want."

Much later, as Taryn laid there and listened to the steady sound of Matt's chest rising and falling, she stared at the empty space above her bureau, where the picture of the Shaker had been just the day before. There was a faint dusty line there now, the space inside bright and clean. She'd swept the glass up and disposed of it herself. Management had told her not to worry; it looked like the nail came right of out the wall.

She shuddered remembering the room's vibrations, the objects sliding to the ground, the otherworldly growling beside her, and the almost-exciting feel of the power that grew inside of her—the idea that her own emotions were feeding something powerful.

"Matt? Do you believe in demons?" she whispered. But his soft snoring continued. He couldn't hear her.

CHAPTER 18

*T*he drive to Lexington was much more pleasant when

there was someone else with her doing the driving. Taryn was able to sit back in the seat, watch the scenery pass by, and fiddle with the radio. She let it land on a station that liked 80's hair metal and let Slash's guitar riffs wash over her. Matt winced a little in the driver's seat. He was more of an Enya person. He lacked both the heavy metal and redneck gene she seemed to possess.

They were there in less than an hour, pulling into the building that looked more like a warehouse than a store. The walkway was littered with old wooden doors, fireplace mantles, windows with glass still intact, windows that lacked glass altogether, and a colorful collection of yard art that included lawn jockeys and frightening gnomes. Taryn couldn't wait to get inside.

The woman at the counter looked frazzled. Her bright red hair was piled on her head with a series of bobby pins, most of which had come loose. There were streaks of solid white coursing through it. She wore an oversized sweatshirt and yoga pants, her feet in heavy duty boots Taryn could see as she walked over to a display and began rearranging a selection of old rusty screws and bolts.

The inside was a collection of color, textures, and dangerously sharp objects. From where she stood she could see endless rows of doorknobs, planters, hinges, and bathroom fixtures. Through another door she caught a glimpse of clawfoot tubs, metal stair railings, concrete steps, and tools. This was her kind of place and made her itch, again, for a house of her own that she could renovate. Taryn had no decorating skills of which to speak but she liked to shop well enough.

"Can I help you?" the woman asked, her voice raspy and deep.

"I don't know where to look first," Taryn confessed. Matt looked like a deer in headlights. He was more of an IKEA person. "I'm so excited to be here."

"Well, we've got more than 8,000 square feet so have a wander. Just watch where you step."

Taryn understood what she meant because in some areas of the store there was literally no place to stand. In others she was looking at no more than a few square inches. She could think of a few HGTV shows that would've gone nuts over such a place.

For more than an hour they wandered through the rooms, Taryn marveling at the architectural salvage and Matt gingerly trying to peek through the old fabrics and dusty bric-a-brac without knocking anything over.

Since she didn't really have anyplace to store anything, Taryn couldn't buy what she wanted (the seat to an old carriage). She didn't want to leave empty-handed, though, so she settled on an antique suitcase that she could screw some legs on and turn into an end table.

At the desk, she rang the little bell and the woman popped out from behind a closed door. "Find something?"

"I would've spent more," Taryn swore, "if I had a way to get it home. And somewhere to put it."

"I know what you mean," the woman agreed. "I own it and want to take everything home myself."

Taryn smiled. She'd found a kindred spirit.

"So what are you doing around here? You live here?"

Taryn shook her head. "Just staying over at the Shaker village and working on a project. I'm doing a reconstruction landscape of three of the old buildings they're restoring."

"Aw, so you're my kind of girl," the woman declared with approval. "I bet you also like crawling in through windows, getting yourself dirty from old wood floors, and taking pictures."

"Yes," Taryn laughed. "Those are some of my favorite things."

After she'd rung Taryn up, the woman stood back and put her hands on her hips. "I'm Lucy, by the way, and I have something you might like. I just got in a bunch of stuff and don't know what to do with it yet. Hold on."

She darted back off but returned momentarily, holding a stack of papers. Upon closer inspection Taryn could see they were photographs. "These came from Shaker Village, actually," Lucy explained. "They're very old so handle with care."

Taryn flipped through them reverently, gazing at the images, many of them scenes from the 19th century, and faded so much with age that they were hard to make out. One caught her eyes, however, and she pulled it back out and studied it with interest. It was a group shot of several people standing in front of the meeting house, most of them with sober expressions, even the children.

Evelyn stood near the middle, hands clasped in front of her. A child stood beside her, trying not to smile. He must've been warned not to act up while they were documented for posterity's sake.

Taryn felt a warmth spread over her; seeing Evelyn again was like seeing an old friend.

A small gap between the men and women had Matt laughing. "They really were segregated, huh?" he asked.

"Yep," Taryn smiled. But when her eyes fell to the other side of the picture she gasped. There Morgan was, clear as day, standing in the middle of the men. His handsome good looks and impish smile was out of place among the stern exteriors. He looked like an overgrown boy, out for a walk, who got caught up in the wrong crowd. Unlike the others, he was beaming from ear to ear, staring straight at the camera.

"Look," Taryn pointed. "There's Morgan."

"You know those people?" Lucy interrupted, coming around and peering over Taryn's shoulder.

"Well, not personally. But I've been studying them a lot."

"That young guy, what did you call him?"

"Morgan," Taryn replied. "He was murdered while he lived there. Obviously after this was taken."

Lucy shook her head, lips pursed. "No, I don't think so. I know a little about the Shakers and there was only one murdered during that time. It was a big deal. His name was Morgan, but that's not him."

Taryn looked up in surprise. "It's not?"

"Nope. That's Morgan," Lucy pointed at a tall, thin man a few people over. He stared at the camera with a steely gaze, his eyes dark and cold. "And he was definitely murdered."

Taryn had no idea what to do with that information. She'd been wrong. It wasn't the first time, but it was still a shocking disappointment.

"Well, if that's not Morgan than who is he?" she asked.

Lucy shrugged. "I don't know but I know someone who might. She's really into all the Shaker genealogy and shit. I got these from her and can give her a call if you'd like. She lives in Harrodsburg and might be up for a visit. If she feels okay."

"You sure you don't mind calling a customer like that?"

Lucy laughed, a rich sound that rattled the selection of jelly jars behind her. "She's not a customer. She's my aunt."

The small shotgun house was painted barn red and boasted

two metal 1940's style chairs on the front porch. A small flower garden had been planted in the front and the flowers were a mishmash of color, height, and types. It was obvious the planter had chosen them because they liked the flowers, not because any thought was given to landscape design. Still, they were neatly mulched and weeded.

Several tomato plants had been started by the porch and were poking through the earth in small clumps. A cucumber vine was beginning its climb up a fence post. Two brightly-colored cushions, both clashing and different colors and fabric textures, somehow made the cold, metal chairs look more inviting.

Taryn liked the house. She could already tell it was well lived-in.

With Matt standing a respectable few feet behind her, Taryn gave the door a nice rap and waited. They were lucky she'd been willing to meet with them that afternoon. "My aunt is a little strange," Lucy cautioned them, "but I like her. I'm the only one in the family who really gets along with her."

"I can understand that," Taryn said. "I had an aunt who was the same way." She thought of her Aunt Sarah, living and dying in that big New Hampshire farmhouse all by herself and shuddered. She should've been there for her.

"Well, at any rate, her bark is worse than her bite so just ignore her if she starts going off on some tangent. She does love the Shakers a lot and can tell you just about anything you'd want to know," Lucy said in admiration. Taryn could tell there was a lot of respect for her aunt.

Taryn was about to knock again when she heard the slow, meticulous, shuffling from the other side of the door. Of course Lucy's aunt was elderly; even in such a small house it would take her awhile to get to the door. "Sorry!" came a fairly-strong sounding voice from the other side. "Got beans on the stove and had to give 'em a stir!"

The sound of several locks being turned echoed on the small porch and then the front door was flung open. Taryn and the other woman were left standing inches apart, on the screen between them.

"Well, huh," the other woman said. "How do you like them apples?"

"Is everything okay?" Matt asked, stepping forward at last.

Taryn laughed. "We've met before. Matt, I'd like you to meet Della...er...Susan."

"Life is just one series of coincidences after another," Susan grinned. "Well, come on in. I didn't expect to be having company but if I throw some cornbread in the oven I think we could have a nice supper. You are staying, right?"

You never turned down supper at a southern woman's house. "Yes ma'am," Taryn answered. "It sounds and smells good."

Hours later, after vast amounts of food had been put away, the

table cleared, and the dishes washed an on the rack to dry (Susan refused to get a dishwasher–thought they were a fad) the three adults sat down in the living room to talk. The space was a tiny one but she'd made the most of it, filling the walls with bookshelves and curio cabinets that housed collections of whimsical unicorns, faeries, and dusty paperbacks–everything from James Patterson to Jane Austen. Taryn felt right at home.

"I *knew* I felt a kinship with you when I met you at the pond," Susan chirped. Matt was in the kitchen, fixing everyone sweet tea, while the women talked among themselves. "You're a girl after my own heart. I didn't realize you were so interested in the Shakers. It's clear this isn't just a job for you."

"I love them," Taryn said simply.

"Do you know why?" Susan prodded with interest. "Are you very religious and pious?"

"Oh, God no," Taryn laughed.

"Good."

"I like the idea of belonging to something," Taryn admitted. "Of being part of a community, or at least something bigger than yourself."

"Do you like being around a bunch of people, then? You don't strike me as a particularly sociable person, no offense. When we were first introduced you were hiding yourself away, as I recall."

"It varies," Taryn admitted. "I like the idea of being around people but sometimes they make me nervous. I have never fit in. Not anywhere. The reason Matt and I became friends in the first place was because we were both kind of recluses, even as kids."

"What about in college when you were studying? It seems like there you would've been among those with similar interests," Susan pointed out.

"I tried. Same with photography and painting. I've joined groups, both online and off, and gone to workshops. Attended conventions. But I've never found one I felt comfortable with. I always end up hiding away in some corner of the room, standing back and watching everyone laughing, bonding, having a good time. It's like looking at a painting, something you can never truly be a part of. People don't notice me and I feel phony with the effort."

"I also grew up this way," Susan smiled. "And it's one of the main reasons I live alone now. The outside world just never felt ready for me. I always found more solace in the trees, by the river, in my garden, in my books...those were the places I was happiest. Those felt more real to me, and places where I could be myself, than in any group setting."

"I know the Shakers had their problems, but they were a part of something bigger, always doing things together, always belonging."

Susan raised an eyebrow. "And when they didn't belong? When things weren't always so rosy and chipper?"

"Then things were bad. Just like anywhere else," Taryn said sadly.

"And that's where we get into our story of Morgan and Evelyn," Susan inserted.

"Evelyn and Morgan?" Taryn asked in surprise. "But I thought the young man in the photograph wasn't Morgan."

"Oh no," Susan said, a secret smile playing at the corner of her mouth. "That's not Morgan; his name was Julius. You'll learn about his fate in a moment. But first, I have something for you."

She excused herself from the room and passed Matt who squeezed past her carrying a tray of hot chocolate. "Everything okay?" he asked, setting the mugs and spoons down on the coffee table.

"Yeah, I think so. She has something to show us she says."

Susan was only gone for a moment and then they heard her slowly shuffling her way back through the rooms, passing through the small dining area and kitchen to the living room. The house only had five rooms: bedroom, kitchen, bathroom, living room, and utility room. But it was all one person needed, Taryn reckoned.

When Susan returned she was carrying a large album. Taryn thought it was full of pictures at first but when Susan sat down beside her on the couch and placed the album between them Taryn could see that it was more of a scrapbook. She looked on in wonder as Susan pulled out letters, photos, and receipts.

"Where did you get all this?" Taryn asked, more than a little impressed.

"My great-great uncle passed them down through the family and now they're mine. At least until I'm dead. I give a little to Lucy now and then. She's one of the few who care about our past."

A photograph caught her eye right away, the unmistakable form of Evelyn standing under a tree, mouth tense, hands firmly placed on the shoulders of the young boy in front of her.

"That's him," Susan said, smacking her lips against the hot chocolate. A little drop fell and spread across her cotton

237

dress. She dabbed at it daintily with a real cloth napkin and then went back to sipping. "That's my great-great aunt Evelyn with my great-great uncle Edward. Weren't they a fine-looking family?"

CHAPTER 19

*T*hese are the only two pictures I have of Evelyn as a

young woman, this one here and the copy of the one from the store. Of course, photography was just getting off the ground back then and once she moved in with her relatives in town the opportunities were gone. She didn't have another one made until her children were out of diapers. This is the only one I have of Edward," Susan explained.

"And Julius? Who was he?" Taryn asked, gently running her finger around the edges of the photograph. It was just a copy of the original but Taryn still treated it with reverence.

"Julius was born at Shaker Village and lived there his whole life," Susan said. "He was an orphan they took in, I don't know where from, and when he was twenty-one years old he took the oath to become a Shaker. He worked on the farm, much like your friend Dustin does now. There isn't much known about him. He would've been a typical member of the order I suppose. He wasn't a deacon or elder or any of that nonsense," Susan cackled. "Just a man."

"How do you know so much about him if he didn't do anything extraordinary in his life?" Taryn asked, sensing more.

"Oh, I'll get to that. In fact, I can show you."

"And Morgan?"

"Morgan was a deacon. You can tell from his pictures that he wasn't happy-go-lucky. Just look at that sour face. He came to Kentucky from an order up in Massachusetts. Has the same name as the college."

"Harvard?" Taryn asked cautiously.

"Yes, that's the one. Harvard. By accounts he'd joined up with his wife and six children. A year or so later she quit and took the kids with her, leaving him behind. I don't know what happened to her. It happens."

"And he was killed," Taryn prodded.

Susan nodded. "Yes, he was killed. Killed in the ice house, in fact."

Taryn shuddered as that particular imagery snapped into place for her: the pale hand reaching out from the rubble of stones, the dirty fog, the cries of pain...Had he been reenacting

240

his death and, if so, how often did that particular happy event replay?

"I thought maybe someone was stealing and he caught them. They maybe hit him in the head or something, like an accident, and left him there to die."

Susan sat there for a second, eyes glued to Taryn, her own face passive. Then she erupted into peals of laughter so hard and so long that Taryn was afraid she'd get choked or dislodge a blood clot. By the time Susan was finished laughing, big booming noises that shook her entire body, tears were welling up in her eyes and she'd worked up a good coughing fit. "Oh, I'm sorry. So sorry. It's just that...well...I suppose you could say it was an accident. But it isn't often that an ice pick will fall out of someone's hand fifty-six times."

Taryn was speechless. An ice pick? Oh, dear lord. Even Matt looked a little pale. That was just slightly too horror movie for him.

"Fifty-six times?" she finally gasped. "So he really was murdered. And, oh geeze, talk about overkill. Why?"

"This is where we need to look back to Mr. Julius here," Susan rapped her fingers on his face.

"Julius killed Morgan?"

"You're not surprised?"

"Well, I mean, I don't know Julius, he's new to me, but it would've shocked me more to find out Evelyn killed him.

Susan snorted. "She should have. The monster."

The next thing Susan handed Taryn was a piece of yellowed paper, folded over many times. "Here. Take a look at this."

Taryn was afraid to open it; it was more than one hundred years old and she didn't want to be the one responsible for damaging it. But her curiosity was great and, after all, she'd come that far.

There was a single piece of paper, the handwriting old-fashioned, sloppy, and male. She struggled to make out some of the words but with Matt reading over her shoulder they were able to put it all together after a few tries. The words broke Taryn's heart.

Dear Julia,

Thank you oh so much for the lovely visit three weeks ago. It was wonderful to look away from the floor and see someone I know, and love, looking back. I know our singing and dancing continued on for many hours and I was exhausted myself by the time it came time to turn in. I can only imagine how uncomfortable it was to sit against the wall on those hard benches.

I only got the chance to speak to you for a brief moment, and was unable to get all of my words out (the walls have ears), but will try to do so now.

Although this is my home, I am no longer safe or welcome here. Edward and I both need shelter immediately and I am asking you for permission and acceptance into your home. I realize we would be quite the burden on you but I am adept in herbal lore and have tolerable sewing skills. I can also help you with your young ones and govern them until they are ready for school if you wish. Edward, though eleven this winter, is strong and a hard worker. He would be no trouble. Indeed, he would much rather have his nose in a book than anyplace else.

I spoke to Mother and Father but they do not want to leave. They have managed to find a measure of peace here and do not want to see it disrupted. They also assured me that neither Edward nor I am their responsibility or duty anymore, that our family is the order and no longer by blood. I shall miss them greatly and it still makes my heart ache to think of the years before joining the Believers, when Mother would sing lullabies to us and rock Edward on her knee. I was once allowed to call her "Mother" and she was everything a child could hope for. She is but a shadow of her former self, however, and I do not know this new person.

I have asked Julius to depart with us. You met Julius in town when he came with seeds and cuttings. He is what brought you to me. Julius is a fine man and honorable. Indeed, he protected me when a man who should have known much better made his intentions known to me and would not think of the repercussions. I adore Julius and could not love him more if he were my own husband. I shall ask again for him to accompany us, but my hope is not strong.

I look forward to receiving your response as quickly as possible.

Yours truly,

E

"You think Julius killed Morgan?" Taryn asked after they'd all had a chance to read, and reread, the letter.

Susan hesitated and then bowed her head. "I believe he did. The violence of the act, or overkill as you called it, was too much. It's obvious to me that there was a relationship between Evelyn and Julius and she admits to as much in the letter. It's also clear that Morgan attacked her."

"I think he did it more than once," Taryn agreed and then told her about the attacks she'd seen at the park, and the ones she'd felt herself.

"Morgan was a terrible man. There are other stories about him that say as much," Susan sighed.

"But the Shakers were so peaceful." Taryn was disappointed. She didn't like to think of a Shaker as an attacker, a rapist. That seemed to be more of a modern occurrence, something that happened in the "real world." Not in the idyllic Shaker village.

"Strong religious settlements and belief groups draw a variety of people, for a whole mess of different reasons," Susan interjected. "And there are many people who adore having that power, especially in a group like the Shakers where they had limited personal freedom."

"And sometimes the members are mentally ill." Susan and Taryn both turned and looked at Matt. He'd been quiet so far. "I'm not saying you have to be crazy to be involved in a religious group," he laughed, holding his hands up in retreat. "I'm just saying that sometimes people are going through depression, have a lot of anxiety, or suffer from other forms of mental illness and religion gives them that outlet to make them feel safe and happier. It's almost as good as prescription medication."

"You just know there had to be schizos there, too. All that waving around and jumping and talking to spirits," Susan theorized. "Half of 'em probably were crazy."

Throughout this discussion Taryn had not mentioned the baby, nor had Susan. Taryn wondered if she didn't know that part of it herself or was just too polite to mention it. If her vision and photograph had been right, Julius had delivered a stillborn to Evelyn. Whose baby was it?

"What happened to Julius?" Matt asked, breaking her thoughts. "Did he leave with her?"

Susan shook her head "no." "I don't know," Susan replied sadly. "He didn't go with her as far as I know. She didn't marry him, at any rate. He's not mentioned again in any of the family documents or stories. And I looked at the records at the park; he's not in anything after the year Evelyn left."

"Maybe he died," Taryn suggested.

"They would've recorded a death; they were good at keeping records," Matt pointed out.

"Then we don't know what happened to him," Taryn sighed. "Poor fellow."

"It seems like Evelyn was the only one who really got out with a good deal," Matt mused. "Except maybe for Edward."

The drive back to Shaker Town wasn't long mileage wise but it was taking forever for Taryn, probably because she'd been out all day already.

"How you doing over there sweetie?" Matt asked, peering over at her. "You need anything?"

"I'm fine," she answered, trying to put on a brave face. The fact was, riding in a car was becoming harder and harder on her. It was difficult on her lower body to be cramped without frequent stretching and the vibration of the vehicle upset her stomach and made it cramp. She'd already learned all the bathroom stops between the park and town.

Matt patted her on the knee and turned on the radio. He skipped over a song she knew he liked and, instead, searched for a country music station for her. When Dwight Yoakam's "Thousand Miles From Nowhere" filled the small vehicle Taryn leaned back and closed her eyes, letting herself get lost in the familiar and comforting twang and melody.

"I have a question," Matt said, turning Dwight down and annoying Taryn in the process. She didn't like for her music to be interrupted when it was a good song.

"Yeah?"

"How would Evelyn and Julius um, you know..."

"People will always find a way to be together if they want," she answered, thinking of the dream she'd had of him down by the river.

"But what about meeting? How would they have gotten to know each other in the first place if they were so segregated?"

Taryn mulled this over in her mind. She finally came up with a scenario that made sense to her. "Well, all the brothers had a counterpart, a sister who washed his clothes, fixed them when they tore, kind of keep him in line and tell on him to a deacon or whatever if he acted up."

"So you think Evelyn might have been Julius'?"

Taryn nodded.

Satisfied with that answer, Matt turned the radio back up again.

The next time Taryn opened her eyes it was pitch black outside and they were starting to travel downhill towards the palisades. "What happened?" Taryn asked groggily. She'd dozed a little and hadn't realized it.

"I must have missed our turn," Matt apologized. "I was thinking about something. Now I'm just looking for a place to turn around."

"There's an old abandoned house down there by the river," Taryn said, straightening up in her seat. Dwight was long gone and now Emmylou Harris was singing about a Crescent City where everyone knew her name and was glad to see her. "You can still see the driveway. It's circular so no problem turning around."

Matt strained his eyes in the dark, trying to peer through the windscreen into the dismal night. "It's *really* dark out here," he complained.

"There, there it is!" Taryn pointed up ahead, off to the right. "Just turn in where you see that break in the trees."

Matt slowed down to a crawl and inched forward, trying to see the narrow path that once passed for a driveway. "Huh," he mumbled. "You sure this place is empty?"

"Yeah, why? It doesn't even have doors." Taryn leaned forward in her seat and unfastened her seat belt. She tried to peer through the windshield but it was just too dark.

"There's a truck up there, see?" Matt pointed. "Kind of hidden in the trees. And I swear I just saw a flashlight."

"It's 10:00 pm, Matt," Taryn panicked. "Somebody's up to something. Just turn around and get out of here!"

"Yeah, okay, okay," Matt replied calmly He was already trying to make a large turn so that he didn't have to go the length of the driveway. "Probably just some teenagers parked out here to get away from everyone. Just because we didn't do it doesn't mean others don't."

Taryn tried taking deep breaths, telling herself that she was paranoid. Nothing was going to happen. Just because someone had already tried to kill her twice in the past year (the third time was just a misunderstanding) didn't mean she was cursed or that it was going to happen again. Still, thoughts of someone cooking meth in that house (and she'd almost explored it, too!) or checking on their marijuana patch or a hundred other things danced through her head. She wasn't anywhere near as young and brave as she used to be.

Matt was completely turned around and starting out to the main road when Taryn was able to breathe properly again. The moon was out now and lit up the pavement ahead of her like a spotlight. Gray slate had never looked better. She had the distinct feeling someone was watching her from the back and what she really wanted to do was high tail it out of there as quickly as she could. She didn't think she'd feel totally safe until she was back at the park.

The "thump" happened just feet from the exit and had them both jumping. It was dull and soft but the sound was unmistakable. "Oh my god, I've hit someone," Matt muttered. Taryn covered her mouth and rocked back and forth in her seat. She was completely useless.

Matt quickly put the car in "Park" and began unfastening his seat belt. "Call 911," he ordered her. "Tell them somebody's hurt."

"What if they try to shoot us?" Taryn shrilled.

"I highly doubt the police are going to do that," Matt remarked dryly.

He was already out of the car before Taryn could answer.

In a daze, she dug out her phone and dialed 911. The dispatch officer promised to send someone out right away and Taryn hung up, both worried and relieved. She could hear Matt talking softly to someone, using the soothing tone he often did with her when she was sad or didn't feel well, and her blood turned cold. Oh God, they *had* hit someone, maybe seriously injured them. But still, what in hell were they doing way out there in the middle of the night?

Leaving the keys in the ignition, Taryn slid out Matt's door (hers was up against a tree) and looked around. Matt was in front of the car; she could see the hairs on the top of his head catching the headlights. Between the brightness and the heat radiating from the bulbs, it gave an optical illusion of his head being on fire.

"There's a flashlight in the glove compartment," he all but barked. "Can you get it?"

It *was* her car. She knew what was and wasn't in there. "No there's not," she sputtered. I don't have a flashlight."

"Yes you do. I put one in there last night. You're never prepared," he lectured her.

The absurdity of the situation struck her as inappropriately humorous. There they were, standing under a dark canopy of trees where they'd probably run someone down, and they were arguing about a flashlight.

Sure enough, it was where he said it would be. He'd also neatly folded her road maps (she refused to have GPS and still liked darting into gas stations to get directions when she could) and had thrown away some of her garbage.

Now Taryn slid from the car a second time, flashlight in hand. "Are they going to be okay?" she called to Matt as she studied the driver-side door. She was having trouble figuring out if she should leave it open or close it—like that was the most pressing matter at the moment. She must have been in shock.

"I think so," he answered. "Can you bring that here now?"

She'd not even taken a step when the sound of footsteps running through the brush cut through the night. "Oh God, oh God. What happened?!"

When Taryn turned, the beam of light she held in her hand focused on the figure who was now just a few feet from her. The look of terror and grief on his face was worse than the shock. He stared in horror at the front of the car where Matt squatted next to a limp figure, gently trying to feel for broken bones without moving them.

Taryn kept the flashlight on the new intruder. It illuminated his face and shone down on him like a beacon. "Dustin?" she asked conversationally, as though they were all simply out for an evening stroll. "What are you doing with that big pipe in your hand?"

CHAPTER 20

*I*t was five in the morning before Matt and Taryn made it

back to the park.

"I'm going to take a long nap and then I'm going to take my easel out and do the last little bit," Taryn yawned. "You get to the point where you know it's just time to go and move on to the next thing."

"And what *is* the next thing?" Matt inquired as he slipped off his shoes and lowered himself to the bed. He ran his hand up her arm and she snuggled into him, her head on his chest.

"There are a few possibilities. Remember that fire that happened at that resort? It was way before either one of us was born, down at one of those islands in Georgia. A rich person's resort, killed something like fifty people?"

Matt nodded. "The Monte Carlo Club. It still pops up every time one of those television stations does a countdown of the worst crowd tragedies or something. But I thought it was gone?"

"It is," Taryn agreed. "They never rebuilt it. That was back in the 1920s and right after the fire the stock market crashed. The decadence and lifestyle kind of flew out the window, too. But anyway, some rich dude has bought half the island and wants to rebuild it on a smaller scale. They contacted me to work with the architect."

"How much of it is left?" Matt asked.

"Almost none of it. It would be a long job, at least three or four months. Good, stable income and I'd get to live on an island for awhile."

Matt opened his mouth and Taryn thought he might protest. If he did, if he asked her to return with him, or said he'd come to her in Nashville, she might turn the job down. She might go with him. That might be what was next. She was about to suggest it herself when he broke her thoughts and said, "You know, I think that's a great idea. And it's not too far away. I could probably come see you at least once. And you could come see me."

Taryn was a little stunned. To see each other twice in three or four months? And it was only about a three-hour drive from Matt, another reason it appealed to her.

But she smiled thinly. "That's what I was thinking, too."

But the elephant in the room, of course, eventually stomped.

"I can't believe it was Dustin and Lydia breaking into the houses and stealing from people," Taryn swore. "I mean, we sat right here in this room and talked about it."

"People slay me," Matt agreed. "We all hide our true faces from the crowd."

"Dustin looked so ashamed, and so petrified for his wife. I just wanted to hug him."

"He's a thief," Matt interjected. "He broke the law. A lot."

"Oh, Dustin and Lydia aren't criminals," Taryn argued. "Not in their arts. Maybe in their actions...Desperate times lead to desperate measures. They'll be out on bail soon and I want to see them."

"You have a soft heart, Taryn. The reason you see your ghosts is because you're sensitive to everyone's plights, including the living."

Taryn sighed. "And I cry and get angry at the drop of hat."

"You take the good with the bad," Matt said. "You don't get to turn one side off."

Taryn settled back into her pillows and closed her eyes. Lydia was in the hospital. She had a slight concussion and broken arm but she'd be okay. NO charges were being pressed against Matt; it was an accident. A guard was stationed outside her door. Dustin was in the jail, although he'd been allowed to visit his wife. She thought they'd be out on bail soon, if they could find someone to post bail. Unfortunately, she didn't think there was anyone in their life who could do it. It was money that got them in the shape they were in in the first place.

"Why didn't they just declare bankruptcy?" Matt asked sleepily. She could tell he'd be out within seconds.

"Dustin said they tried, but the only kind they could get was the one where you have to pay it all back. It wasn't wiped off. And they still couldn't afford the monthly payments," Taryn explained.

"And moving? For better jobs?"

"Their baby is buried here. They have ties to this place that go farther than just liking it and it being home. And with what money could they move? Relocating for a new job means renting a truck, getting a new place, putting down a deposit, turning on utilities...and if you don't have money to start with...."

Taryn was bitter. They were good people, just trying to do their best. They'd turned to stealing out of desperation. But at least they'd worked together; they were a team. And a tiny part of her was jealous of that.

The perfume bottle on her bureau rattled.

"Oh my God, are you okay?" Julie squealed as she ran towards

Taryn. The dining room was crowded but Julie pushed people aside to get to Taryn's table. "We all know everything."

"I'm fine," Taryn assured her. "Nothing happened to me at all. And Lydia will be fine."

"I just can't believe it," Julie moaned. "They're the ones who broke in on me and stole out of my house!"

Taryn flinched. "To be fair to you, it wasn't personal. They didn't know you'd moved. They never would've done that to someone they know."

Julie caved. "Yeah, I know. They're my friends. They felt horrible when they found out and I don't think they were faking."

Andy bustled in at that moment, his voice booming over the low roar of the crowd. "And to think," he lamented to a small group following him. It was a fellow employee right here at Shaker Village who did it to me."

As he slid past Taryn and Matt's table his volume grew. "Of course, they feel terrible about it. They're doing everything they can to make me comfortable."

"I just bet," Taryn muttered. "Of course he's going to milk this for all it's worth."

The hostess seated Andy at the small, two-person table next to Taryn and Matt and she rolled her eyes. "I was really hoping to enjoy my breakfast this morning."

"Oh, did you hear about the terrible thing?" Andy demanded. She thought his southern accent might have deepened a little, like a southern godfather's. "Oh, but of course you did. You were there after all. And to think you are the one who caught them in action!"

Taryn took a bite of biscuit and said nothing. The bread was dry in her mouth and stuck. She had to take a sip of orange juice to get it down but she put on a good front and acted like she was doing nothing but enjoying herself. "It's a bad thing all the way around," she said primly and turned back to Matt and Julie.

"I just can't believe it, he moaned to the hostess. The tables around them had stopped talking, too, tuned into the Andy Show. "So many things they stole! My television, my computer, my tablet..."

"I thought they were just stealing house parts," Matt interceded. "And they targeted yours because it was being worked on and open."

Taryn laughed. It was true; Andy had not mentioned any of the electronics previously.

"Well, the good thing is that insurance is paying for everything and I can stay here, free of charge of course, for the next week," he babbled. "Who knew, though, that the Friday night I was enjoying my one evening at the movies those thieves were cleaning me out. And I get out to enjoy myself so little these days..."

Julie, who had been listening with a disgusted look on her face, frowned. "Hey Andy? When did that happen to you?"

"Two weeks ago on Friday," he replied. "I'll never forget it. The Kentucky Theatre up in Lexington was showing Butch Cassidy and the Sundance Kid that night and I treated myself."

Julie crossed her arms over her chest and stared at him. "Dustin and Lydia were with me that night. I remember because they came over and got me around 5:00 pm and then we all went out to dinner together. I brought my boyfriend with me because they hadn't met him yet. After dinner they came back to my house and we played cards until almost 2:00 am. Neither one of them was ever out of my house."

Someone tittered nearby and Andy's face grew red. Carol, who'd walked up behind Taryn without her knowing it, stepped forward.

"Do you have proof of that Julie? A receipt or something?"

"Well, yeah," she reckoned. "I have the restaurant receipt because Tristan paid. Oh, and my neighbor saw them leaving, too. He was letting his dog out while they were leaving and after what happened to me he was worried and checked in because he didn't know who they were."

"Well, maybe it wasn't that night," Andy sputtered, uncomfortable.

"Maybe you should think about that a little, Mr. Tribble," Carol suggested harshly. "In the meantime, can you come up to my office for a minute?"

"He totally made that up," Taryn said after they'd walked off, Andy's shoulders slumped. "He didn't get robbed at all."

"That's some funny shit right there," Julie hooted.

"The ironic thing is that he didn't lie because he wanted the insurance payoff," Taryn said wonderingly. "I think he honestly did this to get free nights at the park. Dream big, man, dream big."

The women laughed together and continued to make fun of the insufferable man until Matt finally interrupted them. "I don't mean to break up the party but I am really, really hungry. Think we can make something happen about that?"

Taryn knew she'd have her paintings done by the end of the

day. She'd probably need another day for touch ups but if she applied herself properly there was no reason she couldn't have them technically finished.

"I hate to leave you alone," she apologized to Matt.

"It's okay," he shrugged. "I'm going to walk around and take in the sights. Maybe work on a report I brought with me. I'll find ways of entertaining myself, I promise."

It was not a good day for Taryn pain wise. From the moment she woke up her left hand had throbbed, swollen red with inflammation. The only relief she got was when Matt squeezed it, applying just a little bit of pressure. But he couldn't stay by her side all day, holding her hand. Her hip was back to throbbing, too, but she didn't want to take any medication for it. She tried to save it for days when the pain was really bad and sometimes the hard stuff left her feeling fuzzy headed and mushy. She wanted to be as clear headed as possible while she worked.

Despite the horrible thing that had happened the night before, and knowing that both Lydia and Dustin were arrested, the day was bright and warm, the sun shining down without a care in the world. It was true, Taryn thought with some bitterness. The world really did go on no matter what happened. Life was unsympathetic to the plights of others. They all might as well be ants, or the stone in Mother Nature's shoe.

Taryn painted straight through lunch and it was late afternoon before her stomach began to rumble. She ignored it and continued to press on. When she got in the zone, especially when the end was in sight, she didn't stop. Though her hands throbbed, her hip was stiff and sore, and her back was hunched forward from the pain, but she was afraid if she stopped she'd never be able to pick it back up again. She needed to do this.

The landscape on her canvas had sprung to life; it was as detailed as a photograph. The little schoolhouse's open door was welcoming, inviting everyone who wanted to come inside and stay a bit. The other two buildings were structurally solid, ready for work. The green grass spread out before them like a shag carpet, soft and lush. The large canvas, nearly three feet tall, looked ready to walk right into.

Taryn painted furiously, dipping her brush into the blobs of paint over and over again, and blending them with what was already there. The trees were nearly three dimensional, the sky bright enough to feel the sun.

By nightfall she was finished.

She would set up her easel in her room and let the painting dry overnight. There was nothing to do, however. Her job was done.

Walking back to her room, supplies in her knapsack on her

back and her canvas tucked neatly under her arm, Taryn
hummed a little to herself. The song, "Barbara Allen," about the
hard-hearted woman who'd shunned the man who loved her,
causing him to die of heartache.

"'Sweet William died for me today/I'll die for him
tomorrow'," she sang under her breath. It was the same song
she'd heard Evelyn singing. Matt had recognized it as soon as
she'd offered a few lines to him.

"It's a death ballad," he'd complained. "He ignored her
when she wanted him and then, on his death bed, she ignores
him. He dies from heartache, and probably fever, and in despair
she dies the next day for not being there for him in his time of
need."

"Well that's depressing," Taryn remarked. A lot of those
old folk songs were. The majority of them seemed to be about
death or unrequited love.

"Kind of a beautiful song, too," he shrugged. "It's a
double-edged sword to be in love."

She could see the light on in her second story room as
she approached the path that would take her to her building.
Matt's shadow passed in front of the window. She felt guilty for

leaving him alone all day but Matt was an introvert; he liked being on his own. Maybe they could go into town and celebrate. She liked to treat herself when she finished a project and, introvert or not, he might like to get out.

Taryn was parallel with the site of the old ice house when the fog began rolling in again. "Oh shit," she mumbled.

Picking up her pace, she curved away from the group of trees that encircled the hole in the ground and pile of rubble, trying to get as far away as possible. To an outsider it simply looked as though the river fog was rolling in from the fields, up from the water, and had somehow thickened in that one area. Taryn knew the fog was there because it was a living, breathing thing and was drawn to the darkness that lived underground.

Although she was moving as quickly as she could, the dirty fog found her and grabbed at her feet, pulling her. She tried to fight it, to kick at it, but it clung to her and tugged. She was being dragged to the ice house against her will and there wasn't another soul in sight to help her. To protect her work, she dropped her canvas and easel to the ground. The soft thud was a reminder of the physical world and somehow comforting. For a second the fog broke up around her feet, the icy fingers retreating. And it might have been okay. She might have been able to move on from it and return to the safety of her room.

But she needed to know. It would follow her and eat at her until she did.

Like a ghost herself, Taryn glided towards the darkened indention. The trees rose up menacingly, taunting sentries. The warm night was replaced with a chill that was not of this world.

263

Lips chattering, shoulders shaking, and exposed skin turning blue Taryn pressed forward, heading straight to the thickest part where she had no idea what was waiting for her. Her left hand throbbed painfully at her side, sending jolts of pain up her arm. Her legs from the knees down ached, like something was eating her from the inside out. She imagined an army of little aliens, all inside gnawing on her and ripping her tissue and muscles apart to shreds. She faltered a little then and stumbled, threatening to fall to the ground. She caught her balance, though, and straightened. She could do this.

The bubble of smoke down below was so thick she couldn't see the bottom. White with stringy muscles of gray coursing through it, it reminded her of sausage gravy, thick and creamy. It bubbled, as though in a pot, and pulsated. Alive.

Taryn knew fear; she'd had more than one experience with things not from this life. She'd been so terrified she could barely move, both from the dead and the living. But this was different. Whatever was down there wanted her, it was seducing her. The bottomless pit of evil was part of her doing, a combination of her jealousy, her love, her anger, her frustration, her sadness. She knew it because it was like looking in a mirror. Each time a bubble rose to the top and dissipated she recognized something from her past, something she'd tucked away. There was the guilt of arguing with Andrew before he'd gotten into his car, the anger at the cheerleader girls from high school who had not been mean to her but ignored her as though she didn't even matter, the grief of seeing her life flash by without any real ties to anything around her...and then there was the despair. The overwhelming feeling that she was meaningless in the world, that her existence was unnoticed and pointless. That nothing she'd ever done or would ever do would have a single effect on the world around her.

The fog, a living breathing thing, seemed to nod. It understood. "Come with me," it seemed to chant. "Come down to me and you'll be a part of me. You'll never feel this way again. You'll know more power than ever possible in this life."

And for a brief moment she considered it. She saw the uselessness of her life, the fact that she was an orphan in the world who had never truly been loved for who she was, but what she offered others. And she wanted to go to it.

But then she heard the humming. Someone had taken up the words to "Barbara Allen" and was singing it, someone walking through the open meadow. Taryn could see a flash of hair, a wayward ribbon streaming from a bonnet. "Oh Mother oh Mother, go make my bed," Evelyn sang sweetly. "Make it both long and narrow..."

Taryn shook her head, chasing off the bad thoughts and feelings with one movement. The fog retreated then and grew smaller. It was angry with her and scratched at her legs with its nails of barbed wire, but it slithered away, retreating.

The long, pale arm appeared then, as it did before. It waved helplessly from the hole, the painful moans circulating around her. He was beyond help, and perhaps shouldn't have been helped at all. She couldn't save Morgan and didn't want to. Julius, or maybe even Evelyn herself, had killed him a long time ago.

But another figure appeared then, one who stood opposite her. This one did not appear to see her or know she was there at all. Instead, this small, lithe body stood looking down at the ground, rivers of blood streaming down his skinny little arms and legs. He was covered with it, from the top of his curly blond hair to the tips of his old-fashioned shoes. He was a child, but the look of disgust on his face was purely adult.

With one fluid movement, Edward raise the ice pick in the air and threw it as hard as he could, the point slicing Taryn as it flew through her and tumbled into the pit. She felt a stinging where the object had touched her heart.

Edward was smiling now, something grim and satisfied, and walked away.

CHAPTER 21

I'm okay," Taryn insisted. "I actually feel a little

energized.

Matt frowned at her, his normally smooth olive face lined with worry. "I don't know about that. I feel that with every time this happens to you it's eating away at something. Maybe I'm just overreacting."

This time it had been different, Taryn knew. But she didn't want to get into that with him.

"The painting are finished," she said brightly, changing the subject. "I might have to put a few more touches on them tomorrow but I think they're done."

"Well, that's good." But he didn't look convinced. In fact, he was looking at her like she'd grown two heads.

"I can't forget the blood on his face, on his arms and legs," Taryn said at last. "He didn't look scared or guilty. He looked...proud, almost."

"It was his sister after all," Matt relented. "But, man. I guess he didn't learn to be peaceful here."

"I think it happened more than once. And Matt? There was more."

"What else did you see?"

Taryn hesitated. "It wasn't tonight, but when Melissa was over here visiting she used Miss Dixie and took a picture after I fell and dislocated. Julius was there. Of course, we thought he was Morgan at the time...Anyway, seeing me on the ground, crying, I think it confused him. He thought I was Evelyn and he..." She trailed off, unable to finish the sentence. Just remembering it made her flush a little from embarrassment.

"He did what? He came onto you?" Matt pressed.

Why, he's jealous of a ghost, Taryn thought in surprise.

"No, no. He d-delivered my baby."

Matt's mouth dropped open in surprise.

"I know, it sounds crazy. Believe me, if you'd been there it wouldn't have been any less crazy. But the baby wasn't alive when it was born. He had this terrible look of grief on his face." Taryn shuddered just thinking about it.

"Oh dear," Matt murmured. "That's awful. And he really is the park's protector. Although he seems to have taken a unique liking to you. The fire, the fall..."

"Why do you think that is?" Taryn asked.

"Maybe because you can see him, sense him. Or maybe he really does think you're Evelyn."

"I don't look anything like her," Taryn mused, taking a chunk of her red curly hair and studying it. Evelyn had been a small, lithe brunette with a creamy complexion and sweet face. Taryn was thin enough but she was soft, neither fat nor delicate. Her hair hung down to her waist and alternated between being lush, thick, and silky to being frizzy and limp. She played around with cutting it off but liked wearing it in a ponytail and braid too much.

"I don't mean physically," Matt explained. "But you can see him and feel him. You're good at observing people. She must have been, to be a teacher. And you're both orphans."

He stopped then and closed his eyes. "I'm sorry. I didn't mean to bring your parents up."

"Evelyn wasn't an orphan, though. Her parents were here."

"There are different ways of being orphaned. She was abandoned to the world here by the people who brought her into it. And he didn't have anyone himself."

"Like us," Taryn pointed out quietly.

"Like us."

Something deep in the night woke Taryn up but she'd never remember what it was. She rose out of bed, slipped on her house shoes and bathrobe, and tiptoed to the window as though sleepwalking. She wasn't surprised to see Evelyn on the lawn, her long hair flying behind her, void of her bonnet. She wasn't dancing this time, or singing. She was struggling to walk now, her legs moving slowly with the effort. Taryn recognized the pain on the other woman; it's how she often walked herself.

She watched as Evelyn detoured around the schoolhouse and headed to her side of the park. As she grew closer, the soft glow around her body nearly as bright as the lighting bugs, Taryn could see that she hand a hand placed firmly on her stomach. The small mound was barely detectable through the pale nightgown, but Taryn was sure someone would've noticed. Another woman, maybe. It was difficult to hide those things, even in the loose-fitting dresses back then (the Shaker clothing was out of style even for its own time period).

Evelyn would've lived with other women, worked with other people in the order every day. You didn't get alone time as a Shaker. There wasn't a lot of isolation, at least literally so. She must have had friends, mentors, someone...

And yet now she was alone, creeping through the grass with struggle, shaking hands alternating between rubbing the small of her back and stomach. From time to time she stopped, her face contorting with a painful grimace, and then moved on, each time a little more slowly.

She was in labor and all by herself. Taryn could think of few things sadder.

She wanted to go down to her, to help her, even though she knew the outcome and had no idea how to help a birthing ghost. She would've gone, too, but the moment Evelyn neared the barn closest to Taryn's building she dissipated into the air, her ghostly tribulations over with for the moment.

Taryn was not going back to bed, however.

Now, as though pushed by an invisible force, she moved to her supplies. Ignoring her paints, brushes, and extra canvas she pulled out her sketch pad and a charcoal. Sitting in a pool of light formed by the moon shining in through the window, Taryn began to draw.

The hands that created the lines were hers in that she could see them and feel them. The images she created were someone else's.

She drew with a frenzy, going on for hours without stopping for bathroom break or drink. Within minutes she would fill a page and turn to the next, urged forward by an unseen force hell-bent on telling its story. Sweat broke out along her forehead, pooled under her arms and ran down her back and chest. Her mouth dried out, her lips cracked and bled. Several times her vision wavered, grew blurry, and she was all but blinded. Still, she didn't stop. She wasn't finished.

Though her hands and arms tingled and burned, and her back stiffened from her hunched-over position on the floor, she drew with a mania she'd never known. The voices of the past grew around her, the sounds of singing, dancing, feet banging on the floor. Snippets of songs flew past her, small birds seeking an exit and battering themselves against the walls and windows in the process. Laughter, chanting in prayer, crying, moaning, pleading...the Shakers were alive in the room with her, their history engulfing her and smothering her until she could barely breathe. She panted, her heart racing and threatening to jump right out of her chest, and her blood ran cold.

Nearly delirious by the time she finished, with one final stroke she completed the last drawing and then tossed the sketchpad to the floor in exhaustion. She'd filled almost twenty pages of highly detailed images. The room was quiet at last.

"Taryn?" Matt asked groggily. The sketchpad hitting the floor had woken him up. "You okay?"

She couldn't answer.

"What's wrong?"

The sight of her sitting in the floor, her eyes wild, her face pale, and her mouth slacked open would haunt him for the rest of his life, although Taryn would never know that.

"Oh God! What's wrong?" He was at her side in two seconds flat, smoothing her hair back from her forehead, gathering her in his arms and rocking her back and forth. "Baby, are you okay? What happened?"

She still couldn't speak but was able to lift her hand with effort and point to her discarded sketchpad. When he turned and saw the thing she pointed out he nodded and her arm fell limply back into her lap.

Shifting her, Matt pulled her onto his knee and then reached forward, grabbing the binder with his free hand. Neither spoke as he opened it and began to flip through.

The first few sketches were general landscapes she'd done upon arrival. There were sketches of the meeting house, Centre Family Dwelling, several of the barns, a re-enactor at the spinning wheel, another one churning butter. Matt smiled at them and the care she'd taken, despite the fact nobody would ever see them but her.

There were perhaps half a dozen of these first ones and they were all drawn lightly, some with charcoal and some with colored pencils. She took her time with shading, details, and depth. Some were good enough to sell. And then he got to the recent ones.

There was a young girl, holding the hand of a woman with a stern but compassionate face. The little girl was crying, the tears streaming down her face, her small arms outstretched towards a tall, broad-shouldered man. Without compassion he was walking away from her, his back turned, his eyes forward.

And then a young woman, lying in bed, blanket brought up and covering most of her face. A lantern glowed beside her, shedding a tiny amount of light on the book she had clearly sneaked under the covers with her.

The woman a little older now, standing in a classroom, smiling at the children, her face radiant. A young man peered into the schoolhouse window, watching her adoringly.

Dinnertime, long tables full of Shakers who were eating quietly, ignoring those around them. They looked down at their plates of food, lost in their worlds, except for the young man and woman. On different ends of the dining room but both looked up, caught the other's eyes. Small smiles.

Standing together in a field of corn, hands on a stalk. Nervousness etched on the man's face, excited fear. Compassion and love on the woman's, her hand covering his.

Dancing in the meetinghouse. Feet flying so fast they were a blur. The woman with her head thrown back with laughter, elation on her face. Her bonnet broken, a ribbon alight. But someone new in this picture. Hardened features, stern, gaunt. His eyes bore into her from a window upstairs. She didn't know.

A classroom, desks overturned. A clay vase smashed on the floor. The woman a panicked animal, trapped against the wall. There was no face, no body, no legs...only tangled hands that grasped at her, tore.

And the last one. Sitting by the river, water racing below. A hand on her stomach, but not her own. The young man knelt with her eyes closed.

Shakers rarely prayed aloud; they didn't believe that God needed to hear spoken words and thought that communicating with Him through silent pleas worked just as well. They wanted to "walk with God" like they might a friend. Still, it was clear in the last image that both were deep in meditation.

Matt went through these, one by one, and when he was finished

he looked up and searched Taryn's face. Her breathing had returned to a few breaths short of normal and now she fell against him limply. Something angry and foul beat against the window outside, something trying to claw or scratch its way in. They both ignored it. Nothing could touch her when she was with Matt; they created a wall together. It's what they did.

"I need to get you back to bed," Matt whispered. "Come on, try to stand."

Taryn let him help her up but then she made no act of moving forward. "I'm not finished," she said. "There was one more. It's not finished."

He realized then, that she was still halfway in the trance state she'd drawn in. She still felt like she was sleepwalking; she had no recollection of doing any of the sketches.

Still in her house shoes, Taryn walked towards her door and turned the locks. "Taryn? Where are you going?"

She didn't speak, just turned and looked at him with sadness. Matt was too innocent, too trusting. He really didn't belong in a world where such bad things happened.

She was down the stairs and out the door before Matt knew what was happening. "At least let me get the flashlight!" he hollered. She walked on, but slowed down a little.

The pond was up ahead and as they moved through the thick night she thought of the stories of the babies who had supposedly been discarded in it. For a moment she thought she could even hear their cries, the small mews of little ones in distress. But it was just a trick of her mind. There were no babies in the pond; that was an urban legend.

Already at the maple tree by the bench when Matt caught up with her, Taryn was kneeling on the soft earth, the dirt smearing her knees and caking under her bare feet. Somewhere along the way she'd lost her house shoes. With her hands she was digging into the earth under the tree, her nails breaking down to the quick and bleeding. Blood was mixed in with the soil now and she smeared some across her face when her hair fell into her eyes.

"Good Lord, Taryn," Matt yelped. "What are you *doing*?"

"I have to," she replied strangely, in a voice she didn't recognize as her own.

"Well, here, at least use a rock or something," he offered her a shard of limestone. While she continued to dig, now with something stronger, he looked for his own makeshift shovel and found one in a thick tree branch. Together, sweating and cursing, they dug past the top layer, pulling up sod, and then tugged at the wiry roots. Taryn heard rather than felt something pop first in her shoulder and then in her knee but kept on digging, oblivious to the dull pain.

She was the first to feel the brittle hardness. "Wait!" Taryn cried, motioning Matt to stop. He laid his tree branch aside and dusted his hands off on his pajama pants. They were streaked with mud, dirt, and grass stains but for once he didn't seem to mind.

276

"What did you find?" he asked, a little nervously.

"Let me see your flashlight," Taryn demanded. It was the most she'd said in over an hour.

The pale rays of sunrise were starting to lighten up the sky, giving it a smoky appearance. In the field behind them the cattle brayed and chickens chattered. They barely noticed these things.

Taryn gently shone the bright light into the small hole she'd made. Although she'd already felt it with her hands, she still startled a little at the small skull that looked back at her, empty eye sockets blank.

Her instinct was to reach in and pick it up, cradle the small bones in her arms the same way Julius did. Matt stopped her, though, and gently pulled her hand away. He didn't let go. "It's old, Taryn. Touching it might damage it. We need to call someone."

She indicated her approval with a small smile.

While Matt stepped away and rang up Guest Services, Taryn stayed under the tree with the tiny skeleton. It was the only sunrise he had ever known.

CHAPTER 22

*T*he night desk worker at Shaker Town had received a

lot of strange calls during his seventeen years at the park. He'd had people get lost on the trails after a midnight run, get trapped on the roof of their building (he didn't ask), get caught getting busy in one of the buildings they'd sneaked into, and even die. He'd seen food poisonings, broken bones, faintings, marital spats, and custody battles take place right there in the middle of the meetinghouse.

It was the first time anyone had ever called in a skeleton.

They weren't sure whether to call a morgue, ambulance, or museum. It was a confusing time for everyone, with most of the people called to the scene standing around with hands in pockets. When one of the paramedics saw Taryn's blood-streaked face, scratched-up hands, and small dislocations there had been an audible sigh of relief—they knew how to fix *those* things.

Now Taryn and Matt sat on a bench in front of the meetinghouse. Lydia's beautiful, rich voice was replaced by someone who still had power but lacked the passion. They listened to her sing the old songs about simplicity, however, and waited. They were both too tired to go to bed, even though they'd been up for more than twenty-four hours.

The story was mostly complete now: Evelyn and Julius had fallen in love (how chaste it was remained a question); Morgan, in either a jealous rage or just plain meanness, had attacked—probably more than once; Evelyn had a baby that didn't survive birth; her brother Edward killed Morgan (either because of the baby or just the attacks); and the two of them left the Believers.

They still didn't know what happened to Julius.

Taryn was a celebrity now, with most of the park workers paying their respects as they sought her out. She didn't know how much they knew about the ghosts or what kind of role they'd played. They had to know a little since most made a point of saying, "At least now we know who our ghost is and why she stays."

Most of them didn't know about Julius.

"Do you think Morgan will ever leave?" she asked Matt, after Eddie Jay moved on to his horses.

"I don't know," he answered thoughtfully. "I think he has too much anger, too much resentment. Whatever he had in life has followed him in death. But I don't think he's necessarily a menace to the majority of people who stay here. There's a lot of love, a lot of peace. Eventually that will win out."

"They're going to bury the little one in the cemetery here," she said. "I saw the spot. It's a nice one. They let me name him."

Matt looked at her in surprise. "Really? What did you name him?"

"Matthew Julius," she replied. "It didn't seem right that he was under everyone's feet all that time and nobody knew him. He at least deserved to have an identity, if not a life."

The two were quiet now, contemplative. For a moment it was on the tip of Taryn's tongue to say that she was ready to move on, in more ways than one. That maybe what they were doing was more out of habit and obligation than any real love or passion. That they could be soul mates without being together. But the idea terrified her. A big part of her was afraid that by not being with him romantically, she'd lose him permanently, and Taryn didn't think she could face a life without Matt. Taryn knew that comparing him to Andrew and her life with him was wrong. She was trying to stop that. But now even Andrew was becoming a distant memory, something that belonged to another person in another life. Taryn was not the same person she once was. She was changing.

And the way Julius had looked at Evelyn in the schoolhouse...

Matt, for his part, sat next to Taryn and was silent not because he didn't know what to say but because he had too much to say and didn't know where to start. He never wanted to let her out of his sight again, the idea of losing her was soul crushing, the very thought of her was what kept him alive and had since he was a child. He loved her with everything.

But all he could do was start chattering about bourbon balls.

Small footsteps approached them then, and when Taryn looked up she was surprised to see Susan. "Scooch over," she demanded to Matt. Squeezing in next to Taryn. Susan patted her on the knee. "So, turns out the haunted pond thing wasn't that far off."

"Who knew?" Taryn agreed. "But what I want to know is how did it even get started in the first place? He wasn't in the pond, sure, but close enough."

"I suspect someone would've seen Julius with him, if not helped him altogether. My Edward maybe," Susan theorized. "Or just someone too afraid to speak."

Taryn nodded, still trying to process.

"I'm afraid I held something back from you the other day," Susan apologized, reaching into her purse. "If I'd known what I know now I would've shown you then. But there's no time like the present."

"What is it?" Taryn asked, taking the brittle piece of paper in her hand.

"I think it might answer some questions about Julius, and what happened. Go on, give it a read," Susan urged her.

Taryn unfolded the paper and began to read aloud.

My Dearest Evelyn,

By the time you read this you will be on your way to your new life with Edward. Regretfully, I will not be able to accompany you.

I have no recollections of a life outside of the village. I was brought here as an infant and this is my home. Although I question my faith daily, I've known nothing else. I have happiness here, and up until some time ago, peace. None of this compares to what I have had with you. If I were a stronger man I would leave and what we have would be enough. I have sinned Evelyn, and cannot comprehend why you should have to settle for someone like myself. I am no longer pure of heart and mind for you and you deserve so much more than I can give.

The child should have been ours, and I must wonder if God wasn't punishing me for not having the strength to protect you. It has to be me, Evelyn, for He could never do such a thing to you. I will love my son and watch for him, although he is not of my flesh and blood.

I fear I am unable to leave with you or live here without you. A fortnight ago the ribbon from your bonnet broke. I caught it and have kept it in my pocket, feeling its presence with me always. I will now hold onto it, for it will most certainly be my admission to whichever afterlife awaits me.

Yours,
Julius

"Do you think he killed himself?" Taryn asked, handing the letter back to Susan.

"I think that's a pretty good assumption. I mean hell, think about it. Here he was a Shaker, someone brought up to believe his hard work and celibacy would be his ticket to Heaven.

And now he's had impure thoughts, had a baby he claimed even though it wasn't his, and probably helped clean Edward up after the murder. He might have even taken the heat for it; we don't know. The man was on a downwards spiral. And they weren't real forgiving around here."

"His death hasn't been recorded," Taryn pointed out. "So maybe he didn't do it here."

The three of them sat together now, none of them speaking, each one of them thinking of Julius. Finally, Susan broke the silence. "It's a fine thing what your young man did. I approve."

Taryn looked up in confusion. "Did what?"

Matt opened his mouth to protest but Susan cut him off. "He bailed your co-workers out. Went down this morning and paid. They got to go home."

Taryn looked at Matt in shock. His face was beet red and he stared down at his feet, awkwardly kicking at a loose stone. "They were in a bad spot. They needed a break. I just kept thinking about their baby."

Taryn could barely form the words. Even now, there was so much to Matt she would never know or understand. Words were inadequate so she reached over and took his hand. It was cold and smooth in hers.

"It was a nice thing, Matt," she said seriously. "I love you for that."

"He could've drowned himself in the river," Matt suggested in reply. The women looked at him in confusion, trying to figure out what that had to do with Dustin and Lydia.

"Julius? Maybe he jumped in the river. Taryn saw him around there. He couldn've jumped or fallen. Floated downstream. Maybe found by someone else. It would've been a good way to escape, a way to get out without being responsible for leaving."

"He could've drowned himself in the river," Matt suggested. "Floated downstream. Maybe found by someone else. It would've been a good way to escape, a way to get out without being responsible for leaving."

"That's so sad. They were all tormented but the Shakers were all he knew. Evelyn could leave because she remembered another life. Julius didn't. He must have felt like he was kicked out of Eden," Taryn said sadly.

"How about we keep this little secret between the three of us?" Susan proposed. She reached into her purse and took out a tube of bright orange lipstick which she went on to slather expertly across her thin mouth. "You know they'd include the story in one of their damnable ghost tours."

In spite of herself, Taryn laughed. Matt reached over and squeezed her hand, the firmness of his grasp bringing her back down to earth just a little bit. It was the safest she'd felt in weeks.

NOTE FROM THE AUTHOR:

I've been fascinated with Shaker Town since I first visited it as a child, more than 25 year ago. I return almost every year, sometimes just for the day and sometimes to spend the night. Although I have never seen a ghost there, it is reportedly haunted. The ghosts in my book are fictional but slightly based on the kinds of stories that get passed around at the park.

A friend of mine, Thomas Freese, wrote two books dealing with the ghosts of Pleasant Hill. If you visit my website you can find links to those books in my blog. They're a lot of fun and Thomas himself is a former Shaker Village employee.

Although the park in question is loosely based on Pleasant Hill outside of Harrodsburg in Central Kentucky, I've taken liberties with geography and layout. The schoolhouse, unfortunately, is not there. There is a restaurant much as I described it, the site of an old ice house, and a pond. These things are real. Re-enactors really do sing throughout the day in the meetinghouse and you can take a horse and wagon ride through the park. It's also open for visitors to spend the night and, yes, there are lots of ghost stories about the rooms.

Although I talked to numerous people about the Shakers' lives and did years' worth of research (like Taryn, my MA dissertation was on them) there are some things I am sure I got wrong. Hopefully, that won't affect the story too much.

Lastly, the Cowgirl Attic IS a real store in Lexington and I urge everyone to visit it. It's truly unique.

Want alternate endings, chapters from other characters' perspectives, and companion short stories? Join Rebecca's VIP mailing list today at

www.rebeccaphoward.net

OTHER BOOKS BY REBECCA

<u>Taryn's Camera Series</u>

Windwood Farm

Griffith Tavern

Dark Hollow Road

Shaker Town

<u>True Hauntings</u>

Haunted Estill County

More Tales from Haunted Estill County

A Summer of Fear

The Maple House

Four Months of Terror

Three True Tales of Terror

<u>Other Books</u>

Coping with Grief: The Anti-Guide to Infant Loss

Visit her website for ordering information.

<u>Www.rebeccaphoward.net</u>

CPSIA information can be obtained at www.ICGtesting.com
Printed in the USA
LVOW04s1542190815

450752LV00022B/1880/P